# TOAFF'S WAY

ALSO BY CYNTHIA VOIGT

*Young Fredle*
*Angus and Sadie*
*Teddy & Co.*
*Mister Max: The Book of Lost Things*
*Mister Max: The Book of Secrets*
*Mister Max: The Book of Kings*

# TOAFF'S WAY

## CYNTHIA VOIGT

### ILLUSTRATED BY SYDNEY HANSON

ALFRED A. KNOPF | NEW YORK

THIS IS A BORZOI BOOK PUBLISHED BY ALFRED A. KNOPF

This is a work of fiction. Names, characters, places, and incidents
either are the product of the author's imagination or are used
fictitiously. Any resemblance to actual persons, living or dead,
events, or locales is entirely coincidental.

Text copyright © 2018 by Cynthia Voigt
Jacket art and interior illustrations copyright © 2018
by Sydney Hanson

All rights reserved. Published in the United States by
Alfred A. Knopf, an imprint of Random House Children's Books,
a division of Penguin Random House LLC, New York.

Knopf, Borzoi Books, and the colophon are registered trademarks
of Penguin Random House LLC.

Visit us on the Web! rhcbooks.com

Educators and librarians, for a variety of teaching tools, visit us at
RHTeachersLibrarians.com

Library of Congress Cataloging-in-Publication Data
is available upon request.

ISBN 978-1-5247-6536-1 (trade) — ISBN 978-1-5247-6537-8 (lib. bdg.) —
ISBN 978-1-5247-6538-5 (ebook)

The text of this book is set in 11.5-point Goudy Old Style MT.

Printed in the United States of America
August 2018
10 9 8 7 6 5 4 3 2 1

First Edition

Random House Children's Books supports the First Amendment
and celebrates the right to read.

FOR THE ONE AND ONLY TOPHER

# TOAFF'S WAY

# WINTER

# TOAFF IN TROUBLE

*What if I—?*

He leaped. Off the horse chestnut branch and out, into empty air. Gray clouds hung over him, white snow shone below, and it was . . . He thought his chest would burst with it.

Then he landed on a maple branch that sank gently under him. His bushy tail gave him balance. His sharp nails gripped and he ran toward the trunk, where he sat up on his haunches and whuffled. He hadn't known he could do that. Nobody had told him. The pride of it, and the surprise . . . And there was a climb to come, climb up or climb down, whichever he wanted. . . . Sometimes everything was so wonderful that all you could do was whuffle.

A crow burst out from the top of the maple. The bird entered the sky on widespread wings, screeching, *kaah-kaah*. Talking to me? Toaff wondered. But what would a crow say to a squirrel? Maybe *Good leap!* Or *Get back where you belong!* Or could it be saying *Follow me!* as it floated over the pasture toward the woods beyond? Toaff had asked his mother what the crows were saying and she had told him, "They're warning us."

"Why?" he had wondered, and she had said, "Crows take care of gray squirrels."

"Why?" Toaff had wondered, and "They want to," she'd answered, so "How do you know?" he asked, but she just sniffed.

Sometimes Toaff wondered if he was the only squirrel on the whole farm who had questions. He hoped he wasn't.

He watched the crow out of sight before he circled up the maple's trunk, careful to leave a few branches over his head. Everybody said that hawks and eagles and ospreys were always on the hunt, especially on a winter day. No squirrel left himself exposed to danger from above. No squirrel who hoped to live another day.

Toaff hoped to live a lot of another days.

From high up he could see the two long lines of bare-branched maples, marking the sides of the snowy drive. Those maples would make two pathways a squirrel could travel along. They even offered a couple of long-branched connections where a squirrel could cross from one side of the drive to the other, without having to touch the ground. The drive was perilous for squirrels because of the machines, machines that carried humans around and crushed a squirrel without even noticing what they were doing.

No one in Toaff's den left their side of the drive, where their dead pine stood beside two young firs at the edge of a pasture, near to a stone wall and a safe distance from any machine. No one crossed the drive to the woods that grew over there. Everyone knew that their side of the drive was the best place to forage, and the big hollow deep in the dead pine was the best place to have their nests. Their pine had died a long time ago and bugs had burrowed into the soft places where branches had broken off; then woodpeckers had hunted for those bugs, drilling into the wood; and after that, squirrels finished the job of turning the hollow spaces into one large cavern. When Toaff asked his mother, "What's a woodpecker?" she said it was a bird. "Like a crow?" he asked, and Braff said, "Not a bit," as if Braff already knew everything and Toaff didn't know anything.

Braff had never been this far from their dead pine, so Toaff thought he would go a little farther. Whuffling with nervousness and excitement, he made his way down the line of maples. At the fourth tree, where the stone wall separated their pasture from the woods beyond, he saw a long branch that stretched out across the drive meet a maple branch from the other side. *What if I—?*

He leaped.

Once across, he sat up on a branch, entirely on alert. He sniffed the cold air and listened. Were those voices? Was that squirrels talking?

Toaff couldn't see even a shadow moving. But it sounded as if the voices were coming closer, so he ran down the maple trunk to meet them. But these squirrel voices were filled with slow churring sounds, not at all like the quick chuk-chuckings in his own den, and they were quarreling.

"Mine!"

"Mine!"

"Did you see him?" asked an excited voice.

"I saw it first!"

"I got it first!"

"You're a thief!"

"You stole mine yesterday!"

"Did you see how far he jumped?" the excited voice asked.

Toaff stepped forward to greet them and from then on things happened too fast:

Toaff saw a squirrel who didn't have a familiar fat, furry gray shape. This squirrel was small and rusty red. Bright white circles ringed his eyes. Toaff had never seen any squirrel who looked like that, but, he reminded himself, he hadn't been alive very long and there was a lot he hadn't seen. He could tell by the head and tail that this couldn't be anything other than a squirrel, so he decided not to be afraid.

The wild-eyed little red squirrel sat up on his haunches to stare at Toaff. "I saw you!" he said, in that excited voice. "Leaping! It was . . . Can you do it again?"

Before Toaff could answer, other voices broke in, voices as ugly and angry as voices full of soft churring sounds can be. More small red squirrels, too many of them, rushed at him. They held their tails stiff and high and they snarled, "Get out! Get out—now!"

"He was flying!" the first little squirrel said. "Didn't you see?" and Toaff thought that *flying* was a word that soared up and out and across.

"That's exact—" he started to agree.

"We'll bite!" cried the other red squirrels. "We've got teeth! We bite!" they shouted. "Get away! You better get away from us!" They closed in on him, in a crowd, and bared their teeth.

Toaff ran. That was all he could do. They were squirrels and could climb right up a tree after him. All he could do was run. If he could just get across the drive . . . He ran out onto the packed snow.

A loud, grinding machine sound drowned out the snarling voices. Out of the corner of his eye, Toaff saw a machine rushing at him. It came so fast he knew he would never make it to the other side. He spun around to retreat, but that was where all those red squirrels were, and besides, the machine was too close. He knew it. He did the one thing he could do: He dashed ahead of the machine, up the drive, turning so fast he barely had time to breathe. If he could get far enough ahead, he could swerve away to the other side. He had no other chance, he knew.

Toaff ran, and the machine was right behind him, and

he didn't even dare to turn his head to see if he was drawing ahead, it was so close, and so loud, and it was hard enough trying to gasp in air. . . .

He was at the end of his strength. He knew it. He couldn't lift his paws for one more step. The machine was going to roll over him, and crush him, and he would be dead. There was no way to avoid it. He stopped running and curled up, his fat tail wrapped around him as if he was in his nest about to go to sleep instead of lying in snow right in the middle of the drive, waiting for a machine to kill him.

The machine roared—was it glad?—so loudly that all the air around Toaff jammed into his ears and he couldn't hear anything. He squeezed his eyes shut and the air of the machine rushed at him, and all over him. Then it was gone and the machine's roar was moving away along the drive.

Toaff uncurled his tail and dashed to his own side of the drive to hide behind a tree before the machine could come after him again. Too weak to climb, he huddled against the trunk to catch his breath, to stop his shaking, to try to understand what had happened.

Because nothing had happened. Nothing at all.

But that was impossible. He couldn't think, for all the fear still skittering around inside his head, and maybe he saw red squirrels moving in the shadowy woods, across the drive—

Toaff fled.

# THE SQUIRRELS EXPLAIN THINGS

Not until he had made his way back up into the horse chestnut did Toaff know he was safe, and even then he didn't *feel* safe. He felt jittery and uneasy. He couldn't stop thinking, the memories all jumbled up—*flying*, the little red squirrel said; *kaah-kaah*, the crow said; *we bite!* snarled voices; and the huge machine roared. He had to try hard to stop hearing them, or seeing the bright white rings around those squirrels' eyes, and the wide snow-covered drive that separated him from safety. He was working so hard not to remember that he almost didn't notice the way a fine snow had started to fill the icy air.

When he did notice, Toaff scurried down the horse chestnut trunk to scramble up the dead pine and tumble into a familiar, friendly lightlessness. Two voices greeted him. "About time," said Braff. His mother, because she was a mother, asked, "Did you find something to eat?"

Toaff was so glad to be safe in the wide warm den, with its two big nests and its stores of food, that he boasted, "I jumped across. Right through the air. I went from one maple to the next and never touched the ground."

"I already did that," Braff answered.

"A crow was watching me," Toaff added.

"Why would a crow watch *you?*" Braff scoffed. "What's so special about you?" he asked, then answered himself, "I can tell you what: nothing."

So Toaff did what all creatures do when their litter-mates refuse to admire them. He poked his nose into Braff's ear and snuffled, tickling it, then moved down to the soft place under Braff's front leg to snuffle there until Braff couldn't help but whuffle. "Don't *do* that," Braff protested as he twisted around, whuffling, to snuffle under Toaff's front leg, and the two of them became a furry ball wrapped around with thick, silvery tails, rolling about in the darkness and whuffling wildly. Until their mother's voice told them to "Stop that foolishness, you two! Just stoppit!"

They stopped.

"Did you find something to eat?" his mother asked again. "Are you hungry? Shall I find you something in the stores?"

"I can do it myself," Toaff said, and went to the stores, where he picked out a couple of seeds.

"Aren't you going to tell us more about this crow?" Braff asked, to make fun of him.

"I don't know any more," Toaff admitted. "It *kaah*ed, the way crows do, and I think it might have been saying something."

"Crows have more important things to do than talk to a squirrel too young to know that jumping isn't such a great achievement," one of the adults told him.

"I didn't mean just *jump*," Toaff protested. "I meant to say *leap*." But really he was thinking of that wide-winged word, *flying*.

"Same thing," said Braff.

Toaff gave up trying to explain.

He reported, "I saw squirrels across the drive."

A short, sharp silence greeted this announcement. Then, "Were they red?" Old Criff asked.

"They were," Toaff told him.

"Did they have crazy eyes?"

"You mean with white rings around them?"

"Stay away from them, Toaff," Old Criff said. "I'm serious. Those are Churrchurrs. They're vicious, Churrchurrs are, nasty little things."

"They *did* threaten me," Toaff admitted.

"They're dangerous. They hate us," Old Criff explained.

"Why do they hate us?" Toaff asked.

"And we hate them."

"Why do we hate them?" Toaff asked.

His mother had gotten suspicious. "You didn't go across the drive, did you? You wouldn't be so foolish as to go into the woods across the drive, would you?"

While Toaff was trying to think of what to say, Braff was already announcing, "He did! I know he did! Look at the way his tail is curling under him. It always does that when he's done something he knows he shouldn't."

Toaff straightened his tail.

"Why would you do that?" his mother asked. "You *know* better."

"Anyway, I'm back," Toaff said, a little cross now, and especially at Braff. "Do machines hate us too? Because a machine almost killed me but I—"

"Machines don't *almost* kill. They do it."

"But I got away, so that can't be true. The machine tried to get me but it missed."

"Machines don't miss."

"I don't know about you, Toaff," Old Criff said. "Crows that talk to you. Machines that miss you. It sounds like stories to me."

Voices chuk-chukked general agreement about this and Toaff knew it would do no good to argue. He was getting the heavy feeling of only-ness, which was about the exact opposite of the leaping feeling, so he went to his nest. Soaff was curled up asleep there, so he poked her with his nose. For wild animals, there's no floating along on the river that separates sleep from waking. No wild animal has time for yawning and stretching and trying to remember dreams. Instantly, Soaff was awake and alert.

"I leaped!" Toaff told her. "Through the air! And a crow saw me!"

Soaff said, "I could try to do that too. Don't you think? What did the crow do when it saw you?"

"It called something, but I don't know what, then it flew off to the woods beyond." He decided not to risk telling her about the machine and the Churrchurrs. If he told her and she made fun of him, or asked the others if that was possible, he would feel even only-er. "I'm sleepy," he said.

"Our mother says a storm is coming."

"It's already snowing outside. But not much."

"There'll be a storm for sure if Mother says so. It'll get colder, in a storm," Soaff warned him. "We should stay warm together. Mother said a big storm."

# IN THE DEN, IN A WINTER STORM

When Toaff woke, the old tree was creaking and trembling, and the den was filled with squirrels. Snow fell so thickly that when Toaff went up to the entrance to see the storm, the wind plastered his face with cold flakes. He could barely see the short, broken-off branch just over his head. The wind was so strong that even with his sharp nails dug in, he almost lost his footing. He retreated back down into the den.

"I told you," Braff greeted Toaff, although he hadn't. But when you all lived in one den and everything any squirrel said could be heard by every other squirrel, you didn't always pay attention, so maybe Braff had. Besides, even if he had, and Toaff had heard him, Toaff would still have gone to see for himself.

The five little ones in the other litter were just weaned and had not yet been allowed outside. They lived in a constant state of uneasy excitement. Of course the storm was making them especially anxious and squeaky. Braff and Toaff and Soaff had already waited through two storms, so they weren't worried, but the little ones kept asking, "What's happening?" and "When will it end?"

"This is just bad weather," Old Criff told them. "I've been in a lot of bad winter weather and come to no harm, as you can plainly see, and that's because I've always kept plenty of stores handy."

"Do we have plenty of stores?" a voice squeaked.

"Enough," Old Criff answered. "We have enough."

Toaff's mother pointed out, "You can never have enough stores. Not in any season, not even fall. Not if you're a squirrel, and especially a mother, with three fine babies she has to show how to survive, and grow strong and smart. Which is me," she told them.

"True enough," Old Criff said. "There can be rains in spring and droughts in summer. That means not many nuts and seeds to be found and stored, when fall comes. Where there isn't enough, someone is going to starve, so a squirrel always needs plenty of stores—not just to get him through the first of spring, but all year round." He thought for a minute, while the wind moaned around the pine, then, "A smart squirrel never empties his winter stores until the humans start burying their seeds," Old Criff concluded.

Someone disagreed. "You don't have to wait *that* long."

Old Criff had the answer. "Have you ever seen a spring-starved squirrel? I have. Nothing but bones, soaking wet with spring rains and stupid with hunger. And slow. Easy prey for any bird with talons, any hawk or eagle or owl. Or raccoons. Or cats and—"

Frightened squeaking interrupted him. "Cats? What are cats?"

"Can talons get into our nest?"

"Will a raccoon eat me?"

Toaff was wondering about that word, *owl*. *Owl* should be a friendly word, not the name of a raptor who hunted to kill. By the sound of him, an owl should be a creature who liked squirrels, not one who wanted to rip them to pieces.

"You little ones are safe in here with us," Old Criff promised them. "But when you're outside? Remember this: Outside's dangerous. When you go out to forage for yourselves, there'll be danger from above and below, danger from any direction."

"Tell us a story, Old Criff," said Swuff, and "Yes, tell about the squirrels swimming," Duff agreed, and the dim air in the den got quiet as the squirrels got ready to listen.

"Long, long, long ago," Old Criff began, in his storytelling voice, but he was interrupted by squeaks.

"I see a cat! In our entrance!"

"I don't want there to be cats!"

"There's just two of them on the farm," Toaff's mother's soothing voice said. "One white, one dark."

"I saw another one," someone told her. "It came out of the big white nest with the dogs."

"Dogs?" squeaked the babies, and now Toaff was curious, too.

"What's dogs?" He couldn't imagine what would have a name like *dogs*.

"Nobody has to worry about being caught off guard by

a dog," Old Criff announced. "They're so loud, you always know where they are. Big clumsy things."

"Have I seen one?" Toaff wondered.

"You wouldn't, not when there's all this snow in the pasture. Dogs stick close to humans and humans stay inside in winter. But you might have heard them. Yarking away to one another, although what anything as loud and clumsy as dogs have to talk about no one knows."

"I've seen a dog," Braff boasted. "It was big. Really big. Bigger than . . ."

While Braff was trying to think of what a dog was bigger than and Toaff was suspecting that Braff wasn't telling the truth, a long, howling gust of wind silenced them all. It wrapped itself around the dead pine and pulled. The tree groaned. A few flakes of snow were blown all the way down into their den. Then the gust was gone. Where had that wind come from? Toaff wondered. Where was it going? He wondered, "How big is the farm, does anyone know?"

"Are you going exploring, Toaff?" Staif whuffled. "What do you think you'd find?"

"I'll tell you what he'd find," Duff answered. "Cats and Churrchurrs, hawks and probably even—if he's really unlucky—the fisher."

Toaff had never heard of the fisher but he didn't like being whuffled at. "There are so many trees on the farm, I could jump from one branch to another and never have to go on the ground. I know how to do that."

"There's nothing special about that, Toaff," the other mother said. "You're a squirrel and squirrels jump."

"You mean he's a *gray* squirrel. Everyone knows that Churrchurrs can't jump. Not like us. Churrchurrs hop," and Duff sputtered into whuffling. Whuffling voices echoed her, "Hop-hop-hop."

"Their pointy ears bobbing."

"The hairs on their pointy ears waving, hop-hop."

"Hippity-hoppity," whuffled Staif, "all the way back to their burrows. That's where they live, in burrows! Underground!"

"They hop? They burrow? They can't be squirrels—I know, they're rabbits!" *Whuffle, whuffle, whuffle.*

Old Criff's voice cut in. "Churrchurrs are no whuffling matter. They hate us. I've heard it said"—and he lowered his voice, as if fearful of being overheard—"they'll eat gray squirrels."

Now Soaff squeaked too.

"That's right," Grief said. "They'd make short work of a little thing like you, Soaff."

"No Churrchurr could get *me*," Braff said.

"You'd be surprised. Those Churrchurrs gang up on their victims."

Toaff, who had met real Churrchurrs, didn't disagree.

"They're so lazy, they'd rather steal than forage," Old Criff announced.

But didn't all squirrels steal the stores of all other squirrels? That was why middens were hidden under leaves or dirt. That was why stores were kept close, in dens and dreys, wasn't it? But Toaff knew better than to wonder out loud about that.

"If you find a Churrchurr on his own, he'll run fast enough," Old Criff announced.

But that first little red squirrel had seemed to want to talk.

"They're cowards as well as sneaks. I'm proud to be a Gray," Old Criff announced.

At those brave words, the wind howled more loudly and the pine swayed. The floor of their den tilted away from underfoot. Stores fell out of their piles and rattled onto the floor. The squirrels braced themselves, nails dug into the soft wood. They looked around at one another. Now that they weren't talking, they couldn't help but hear how fiercely the wind stormed.

The littlest ones were too frightened even to squeak, but their fear made the dim air shiver.

One of the adults spoke, in a calm, calm voice. "A dead pine doesn't have needles on its branches for the wind to pull at. Our den is right in the middle of a dead pine. You couldn't be in a better place in a winter storm. We have big soft nests, lots of stores, and strong pine walls all around. Settle down now. Everyone curl up warm."

So they all nestled down into a sleep as dark and deep as their den.

Until the darkness cracked.

Until over their heads and under their nests, the darkness exploded.

# EVERYTHING CHANGES

Silence woke him. The thick, dark silence seized him by the tail, jerked him up, dropped him down, hard.

Toaff didn't open his eyes. It was wrong enough to hear nothing; Toaff didn't dare to open his eyes and *see* nothing. Or, worse, to open his eyes and see something horrible that had finished off a whole den of squirrels and was now waiting for him.

At that thought, his eyes burst open.

The light told him it was morning, but except for that everything was different, and wrong. There was the wrong amount of light in the den and it was coming from the wrong direction. The round entrance was in the wrong place. There were no squirrel shapes waking up all around him, and no squirrel voices chittering and chukking.

No sounds came from outside either.

Toaff did not move.

Something was wrong with his nest, too. His nest wasn't thick and soft and—he shifted, twisted to get his paws under him, but why did it hurt to move?—and then he remembered. There was a black cracking of the darkness, and he was thrown sideways, and he heard frightened chukking as he tumbled over, falling backward. But after that, nothing. Not one thing. After that, everything was as black as sleep.

Toaff shook off crumbled leaves and began to wonder: Why was the den empty? What had happened to all the squirrels who lived there with him? Had something bad happened to Soaff? He scrambled to the entrance, and he had to go down, not up, to get outside. What could change up to down?

Whatever it was had also moved the broken stump from just above the entrance to just below it, which *did* offer Toaff a good perch from which to look out over the pasture. He scrambled out onto it, and stared.

What he saw first, and mostly, was snow. What wasn't buried under snow was piled high with it. Even the bare limbs of the maple trees, and the horse chestnut tree, too, had thick lines of snow lying along them. Fresh snow weighted down the wide branches of the evergreens, bright white against a green so dark it looked black. A silence as heavy as the snow lay over everything.

Toaff sat up on his haunches on the broken stump, forelegs gathered up against his narrow chest, and listened. Nothing. The storm had blown away all the usual sounds of a winter morning. Then a crow that had been perched high up in the horse chestnut *kaah-kaah*ed and flew off. He watched the bird soar over across the pasture toward the humans' big red nest and wondered if it was showing him where everyone else had gone. Without him.

Branches and twigs lay scattered about, black dots and lines on the snow's smooth white surface. Two thick maple limbs had been ripped off and tossed down onto the pasture. When Toaff looked up over his shoulder at his own tree, he understood exactly what had happened: The pine had been broken in half. The tree had snapped at a point that used to be below their entrance and now its long upper trunk, where their den was, slanted down to touch the snowy ground. This made a long path Toaff could run along to get down. Or—he looked backward and upward—he could climb the short distance up to the break, where jagged blades of wood stuck up into the icy air.

To see more, he scrambled up to the break. He wondered if anything had happened to the humans' big white nest, but it still had the same square shape and stood on the same spot. He was glad to see that the two apple trees were also unharmed, except that the little round fruits that had been clinging so stubbornly to their bare branches had disappeared. Blown off by the wind, he guessed, and buried in the snow. He could sniff out those apples, if he wanted to, and he thought he probably wanted to. Looking out from the ragged top of the broken pine, Toaff wondered where the others could have fled to. How did they manage it, in the storm, in the night, with those young ones to carry?

He wondered, but he didn't worry. Once a squirrel has learned to forage, he knows his mother is ready for him to leave her nest and forget all about having a mother. It might feel strange being alone like this but it didn't feel wrong.

Toaff stayed there on the stump until well into the morning, but he neither saw nor heard nor smelled any sign of squirrel. No machine moved, no human appeared, and no fox came to dig out a buried body. Just the occasional crow was up and about. Eventually, Toaff went back inside, where what had once been the floor was now the ceiling and what had once been the ceiling was now the floor.

He ate some seeds and then tidied the scattered stores together into piles. He wove a new nest out of bits and pieces of the old ones, which was easy to do since this new nest just needed to be big enough for one. When he was satisfied that the den was in order, Toaff went back outside, to consider the best way to get to the apple trees.

# A FOX ON THE HUNT

Toaff didn't waste time feeling sad, or lonely. Squirrels are adaptable. They can live alone as easily as they can in packs or families. They are comfortable in dreys perched high up in tall trees and in dens deep within the woody hearts of trees. Some even live among tree roots or under thick bushes in burrows. They are mostly concerned with hunger. They have to be adaptable about food, too. They will eat nuts or seeds or fruits or vegetables, all with equal pleasure. They will even, if they are hungry enough, eat the bitter new buds of early spring; and if they are starving, and there is nothing else, they will eat some small creature, a lizard, a tiny snake, a bird's egg. A squirrel needs a safe nest and food. Like any other squirrel, Toaff had adapted to all the changes without thinking much about it. What he was thinking about was apples.

He looked at the two trees, and the snow piled around them where the last apples had probably fallen. He considered his path across the distance between where he was and where he wanted to be. It wasn't smart to spend any more time than you had to out in the open, he knew, and it also wasn't smart to try traveling through firs. In a fir, a squirrel could easily lose his footing and fall, tumbling, through the floppy branches until he smacked down into the snow. That's if he was lucky, because if he wasn't lucky he would smack down flat onto bare ground and risk serious injury. Toaff decided to risk a run along the ground, from the protection of a fir trunk to the stone wall that made a long, humped path of snow to the apple trees.

He scurried across to the trunk of the nearest fir and climbed out onto a low branch. From there, Toaff peered out through the branches and listened. He waited until the branch stopped swaying under him and the heavy snow he'd disturbed had plopped down onto the ground below. Then everything was silent again, and still. He waited a few heartbeats more, to be absolutely sure it was safe to descend to the snow and make a dash for the stone wall.

It was a good thing Toaff did that because just then there was distant movement on the snowy surface of the pasture. An animal. A large animal. As it came closer, he saw the long-nosed head, the white chest and rusty fur. It had to be a fox, a fox on the hunt. If a fox caught a squirrel on the ground . . .

Toaff didn't move.

The long legs stepped delicately, the long tail was held low, and the fox's ears were cocked forward, its nose lowered into the snow. The fox left paw tracks and a shallow nose-trail as it glided along the top of the snow, light as a squirrel, intent on whatever it was tracking. Toaff didn't move a muscle. He couldn't see any creature fleeing across the snow ahead of the fox, and *he* certainly didn't want to become the prey. This fox looked thin with winter. Motionless and silent, Toaff watched.

What came next happened so smoothly that Toaff couldn't be sure where one thing ended and the next began: The fox halted. Its forepaws dug into the snow, digging down until its head was hidden and its haunches stuck up into the air. The fox's head came back up holding a small brown mouse in its teeth. The mouse gave one shrill, terrified shriek. The fox tossed its head up and opened its jaws and the mouse disappeared into them. Then the fox loped off.

That mouse must have been tunneling under the snow. For an apple? For some squirrel's buried nuts? That mouse must have felt safe under its thick cover of snow. It felt safe but it wasn't. You were never really safe unless you were curled up in your nest in the hollow of a tree. At any other time a predator could fall on you, and snatch you up.

*Predator* was a word with long dark wings and sharp talons, while *prey* was a quick little word, helpless as a mouse. Toaff knew that a squirrel was prey, and he didn't question it, because what was the use of questioning something like that? But he didn't forget the way that mouse had cried out. Remembering changed nothing and he didn't *really* remember. Just, he didn't forget.

Toaff gave the fox time to get far, far off. He watched it jump over the mound of snow that was the stone wall at the pasture's end; he saw it run into the woods beyond. He waited until he could no longer see even a tiny moving spot, and he was about to descend for his dash to the nearby stone wall when he was halted a second time.

"*Yark! Yark!*"

Dogs? He looked in all directions. Where?

He listened closely, because Old Criff had said the dogs were actually talking.

Did he hear *jump* and *snow* among the yarks? He thought he might have heard those words. Why couldn't he see any dogs?

Voices were speaking together, it seemed, dogs and humans. Then the human voice said something and one of the dogs might have said *in* and what the other said sounded like *house* and all the voices faded away. Did *in* go with *house*? Was *house* an inside thing, the same thing as *den* or *nest*? If the humans and dogs lived together in the big white nest, they might have their own name for it, and that name might be *house*. It would have to be something with an in, like a tree with a den in-side. He would have liked to have actually seen dogs, Toaff thought, as he once again waited for silence, so he could continue on his way to the apple trees.

# BRAFF CLAIMS THE STORES

The apple Toaff sniffed out from beneath the snow below the apple trees was frozen solid. He scraped at it with his strong teeth, but he wasn't hungry enough to make it worth all the effort. It was too big to take back to his den, so he buried it under the snow again. Then he climbed up to the safety of a branch, just to look at the humans' nest. Was it a *nest-house*? He noticed bare branches peeking up over it, the tops of trees at least as tall as the maples along the drive. But he didn't even think of crossing the snowy spaces to find out: A squirrel moving on top of snow is much too easy to see. Toaff was curious but he wasn't silly. He retraced the path back to his den, where there were piles of stores to feed from and strong pine walls all around him.

As he stepped up onto the tip of the pine's trunk, Braff emerged from the entrance. Toaff ran up to him. "Hello, hello!" he greeted his littermate, and at the sight of Braff's cheeks, swollen out with chestnuts, and the furious chewing of his mouth, he couldn't help whuffling.

Braff swallowed and glared and demanded, "What? Just because you're not dead, you can't keep all the stores.

They used to be mine and they still are. They're as much mine as yours, and you can stop that silly whuffling."

"Okay," Toaff said, and he did. "I didn't expect to see you," he said. "Where are you—?"

"So you agree I can take from the stores," Braff said.

"There's plenty and I just found—"

"It smells like you're alone in there," Braff said.

Toaff nodded.

"You better come back with me," Braff told him.

Toaff shook his head and did what he always did when Braff got too bossy. He stuck his nose into the soft place just beneath his littermate's front leg.

"Stoppit!" Braff cried, backing away.

Toaff ignored him, and kept snuffling, to make him act normal again.

"I said stop!" and Braff nipped at Toaff's ear.

"What—? Why did you—?"

"I warned you," Braff said.

"You bit me!"

"I *told* you to stop. I don't play games anymore."

"Well," Toaff said, and began to circle around Braff to go in and get a few seeds for himself. "I've stopped."

"Then let's get going," Braff said.

"I'm staying here." Toaff didn't want to go anywhere with Braff.

"Hunhh," said Braff. "When you change your mind I won't be here to show you where we are."

"That's all right," Toaff said.

"We're right behind the humans' red nest."

"You're there? But it's across the drive, where the Churr-churrs—"

"We're not near Churrchurrs, we're beside the sheep, which before you ask I can tell you are huge and smelly. They're in a pen and you don't have to ask about that either. A pen's like a den with no top and no real walls. Some rabbits live in those same woods and they told us what the pen is and what sheep are and how the humans put out food for the sheep and we can take it. Sheep aren't dangerous if you move fast."

After that announcement, Braff ran past Toaff and down the broken pine trunk. Standing on the snow, tail raised, he turned to call up, "Another snow coming, everyone says. What're you going to do when the stores run out?

It's not long until spring, they say, but still. You don't know the half of what will happen in spring, Toaff. And I don't think I'm going to tell you."

Toaff remembered quite well hearing about the starvations of early spring. "Maybe you shouldn't come back," he called down.

"They're mine, too," Braff said.

"Not anymore. Not when this isn't your nest they aren't."

"What if this next snow is a winter storm again?" Braff asked. "And this old dried-up pine breaks again?" He ran off without waiting to hear what Toaff might answer.

Toaff watched him go and wished it had been Soaff, not Braff, who had come back. He'd be happy to share his stores with her. Was there a storm coming? He sniffed, and did notice the smell of snow. So he wasn't surprised when, in not very long, the air filled with fat falling flakes. This was a snow that filled the entire sky, without any windy threats. All afternoon long and all night long, too, the quiet snow kept on falling.

Toaff slept undisturbed and woke the next morning to a clear sky above and more snow below. There was now so much snow that it muffled the sound of the machine as it pushed snow up and down the driveway, changing a frightening roar into a friendly rumble. When that machine finally went away, Toaff could perch out on the broken stump below his entrance, in warm sunlight, eating a chestnut.

Looking out over the pasture, his fur warmed by the sun, peering across the two lines of maples toward the Churrchurrs' woods and then looking the other way, to the woods beyond the pasture, Toaff wondered about spring. He had heard about one season following the other, spring after winter, summer after spring, fall after summer, and the next winter after that, but he knew little more of the other three seasons than their names. Winter was the one season he'd been alive in. How would he know it was spring? When spring had happened, would everything change, the pasture and maples and drive? Would spring come roaring in, sudden as a storm? Or did it creep in, like a hunting fox?

Toaff didn't know anything, really, not about the seasons, or about the best ways and places to find food. He didn't know anything and there was no one to ask. Should I have gone with Braff? he wondered, but as soon as he'd wondered that, he knew better. And as soon as he knew better, he felt better. He guessed that when spring arrived, he would find out everything he didn't know.

# ICE! DOGS!

The next day, much to Toaff's surprise, what fell from the sky was not snow, but water. All day long a heavy, steady rain drummed down onto the broken pine. Curled in his nest, Toaff listened to its beat and slept. The cold didn't come back until far into the night, but this was a cold so sharp that Toaff burrowed deeper into his nest and wrapped his tail more tightly around his body. In the morning, when he stood in his entrance, Toaff didn't know *what* he was seeing. Each branch of each tree, even the smallest twigs, each needle on each pine, and the whole white sheet of snow on the ground, everything, everywhere, glimmered in sunlight, and glistened and glowed; everything was entirely different and new. After a whole rainy day of sleeping followed by a long night's sleep, Toaff was more than ready to be outside. He jumped down onto the glistening pine trunk—

All four of his legs shot out from under him. Nails scrabbling for a grip, he slid on his belly, slithering down, going much too fast. More than once he almost flew off the trunk to crash onto the ground. His small sharp claws, clutching at the cold surface, could do no more than slow his descent.

"*Yark, yark*," he heard, and "Run!" He was sure *run* was the word he'd heard. "*Yark* play!" and he recognized *play*, too. He heard and understood "*Yark* of ice!"

Ice? Toaff didn't move. He lay on his belly where the tip of the trunk touched the ground. He dug his nails in—dug them into ice?—and waited.

Two animals came onto the drive just in front of the nest-house. What might they be? Dogs, maybe? Probably dogs, Toaff hoped. They were definitely yarking. The bigger, black-splotched one held his legs stiff to keep from slipping, but they were *so* stiff that his back legs caught up with his front legs and he tipped over, landing on his muzzle while his legs scrabbled helplessly at the shining surface of the snow. "*Sturf, sturf*," said the smaller, brown one, and "Not funny!" the bigger one answered.

Toaff could understand them! He could understand what the dogs said!

"Sorry," said the smaller dog. "Dig *yark* nails *yark* ice, Angus," she advised.

Was *Angus* a name? Or was this an angus, not a dog?

"See?" The smaller one lifted a leg to show her nails and then *she* slipped over sideways, crashing down onto her back. Her legs waved in the air. "*Sturf, sturf*," she said, from upside down.

"*Yark* inside, Sadie," said Angus.

Toaff decided *Sadie* and *Angus* could both be names.

The animals were definitely yarking, so they couldn't be anything but dogs, two dogs named Angus and Sadie. He watched Angus move back toward the nest-house, legs stiff, nose pressed down on the snow-ice to keep from falling.

"I smell *yark*," Sadie answered.

"*Yark*, Sadie! Come on!"

"—*yark* smell *yark*. Smell furry," Sadie said, and then turned to slip and slide back toward the nest-house. "Ice!" she yarked. "*Sturf, sturf. Yark?*" she called back.

Toaff had heard the word but it wasn't until she was out of sight that he understood her question: "Squirrel?"

"Yes!" he called. "Yes! I'm a squirrel!" But she was gone, and maybe that was a good thing since he didn't know how dogs felt about squirrels. If, for example, a dog would hunt a squirrel down, and eat him. He had a pretty good idea what Braff would say about a squirrel trying to attract the attention of a dog. What he wasn't sure of was if this was something Braff really knew or something he just pretended to know.

Toaff understood—of course he did—that a smart squirrel would go back up to his den. He understood it as well as if his mother was right there reminding him. But he also wondered what it would be like to slide along the ice.

*Slide* was a word that went on and on before abruptly ending, as if its paws had gone out from under it. Toaff could imagine how it would feel to slide along the icy surface, almost as if you were a bird slipping through air. His nails could always stop him, there was no danger in sight—unless from the sky? He looked up, and around, and the sky was empty.

*What if I—?*

*Whoosh!* With one push he was away from the trunk—

And his legs were splayed wide and he was snout down on the ice. Cold, it was cold, and he needed to pay better attention, to be sure not to go too fast, and to be ready to stick his nails into it. He saw that he had already slid farther from his tree than he'd planned to go. He was so far away that he might not be safe. He spun around to—

*Thunk!*

Toaff lay on his side on the ice. Surprised and unhurt and whuffling. *Whuffle,* and he gathered his legs under him again, slowly, *whuffle,* moving as cautiously as Angus. He pushed off gently, gently, with his hind legs and slid forward. He was heading back to where the pine's tip was buried in the snow, moving easily now along the ice.

But when he got there, he still didn't want to go back into his den, back to sleep, so he turned around and slid out over the pasture again.

For a long time Toaff went back and forth, sliding away from and slipping back close to the pine. When he had finally had enough, he climbed very carefully, and slowly—because he *really* didn't want to slide off the trunk and smack down on the hard, icy ground—up to his den. There, he ate three mouthfuls of seeds and a plump chestnut, then curled up in the nest and fell asleep, in contented exhaustion.

# TOAFF CROSSES THE DRIVE AGAIN

A day later, the sun began to melt the ice, and in not many days it was gone. The drive had turned to dirt. The few patches of snow that remained weren't even deep enough for a mouse to tunnel beneath. Clumps of last fall's grass made brown mounds on the pasture, the days seemed longer, and the nights gave up some of their cold. Was this spring? Toaff wondered. There was a thin little promise of *something* in the air, maybe in the smell of the ground, maybe in the color of the sky.

Whatever the something was, it made Toaff restless. It made him not want to go to sleep because then he might miss what might be happening. It made him want to run along the stone walls to explore everything—the pasture, the woods beyond, the tall trees he could just see over the top of the nest-house. It made him want to leap. He sat on the broken branch and considered the long leafless branches of the maple trees that lined the drive.

*What if I—?*

It wasn't that he had forgotten Old Criff's warnings about Churrchurrs; he just didn't bother to remember

them as he leaped through the sun-filled air from the chestnut into the first maple tree, heading along the drive.

On the long leap across, Toaff was really flying, almost.
The maple branch he landed on swayed under him and
he used his tail for balance as he ran along it. There were
mostly pines and firs in these woods, so Toaff went along
the ground. He dashed from the protection of one trunk to
the shelter of the next, and it was not long before he heard
those voices again, the soft chur-churring voices he remembered. Then he did climb up a thick spruce trunk, although
not far. He chose a low, thick branch and crept out along it
until he could see but was still hidden.

Little red Churrchurrs scurried in his direction, foraging, chattering to one another, sitting up to chew and
look nervously around. Here in the shadowy woods, a few
patches of snow remained unmelted. Here in the woods,
there was not much light, and the air was chilly. The Churrchurrs were scratching at the frozen ground to locate the
middens where seeds and nuts had been buried in the fall.
"Cold," they said, and "Hard as stones," and "Here, I put it
here, right here. I know I did."

"Some thieving Chukchuk must have taken it," a voice
suggested.

"Could be a mouse, they're no better than those Chukchuks," another answered.

"Do you hear something? Is that a coyote?"

"Don't be such a scaredy. You're always hearing
coyotes."

"I wish you'd start hearing the fisher," a voice whuffled. "That would at least be useful."

"You're back!"

This voice came from overhead and it came from too close. Toaff tensed, ready to run, but "I remember you!" the voice cried. "I've been practicing!"

Toaff looked up.

A little red squirrel ran out along a branch near the top of a nearby fir. Light as he was, even lighter than Toaff, the branch sank under his weight. He looked at Toaff and the white circles around his eyes made him look dangerous, possibly crazy, certainly capable of just about anything. "Watch this! Watch me!" he cried as he gathered himself to leap out, across to Toaff's spruce.

"No! Don't!" Toaff chukked. "You can't see—"

The little body flew out into the air. At the same time, voices rose up from below.

"Is Nilf doing it again?"

"Never mind Nilf. I think I heard—"

"Will he never learn?"

"Look! Look there! In the spruce!"

The little squirrel had landed in the spruce, but the branch he'd chosen was too thin. The tree was so thick with needles that he couldn't have known. In fact, there was no branch in the spruce strong enough to stop a falling squirrel. Toaff didn't know what to do. But what *could* he do? And the Churrchurrs were already coming after him.

"It's a Gray!"

"Come to steal our food!"

"Get out, Chukchuk! Get out before we hurt you! We're not afraid!"

Toaff backed up along his branch, but he couldn't take his eyes off the falling squirrel. Toaff watched him—twisting and turning and reaching his paws out, trying to grab—tumbling down in a shower of needles, falling down, down—until he crashed onto the frozen ground and gave a single strangled cry.

At that sound, the Churrchurrs forgot about Toaff. They ran to the fallen body and put their noses to it. "Dead," one pronounced.

With no snow to cushion him, the fall had to be a bad one.

"He can't be dead. Nilf? Wake up!"

"See? Dead. I told you."

"He doesn't smell dead to me."

"He looks it."

"Wake up, Nilf!"

"Let's get out of here. We're not safe, I can tell, I can feel it."

"But I see a holly bush so it has to be—"

"Look at Nilf if you don't believe me."

"Maybe that bush marks the *end* of our territory."

"We shouldn't be here," they said then. "Not safe," they were saying to one another as they disappeared in among the trees. "Should have known better."

Toaff stayed where he was, looking down at the silent body.

But *was* the body silent? Didn't he hear tiny sounds coming from it? Or was that the trees creaking? Toaff wondered if he had to go down and find out. If the Churrchurr wasn't dead, he would go back to his nest and Toaff could do the same. But it might have been his fault that the little squirrel had tried to leap when even Grays knew Churrchurrs weren't good jumpers. Could Toaff just abandon him?

He moved cautiously down the trunk to the ground, listening to hear if those other Churrchurrs were returning, because if they were, he wanted to get out before they got him.

# INTRODUCING NILF

The little squirrel was definitely the source of those noises, and he was moving now, too. He struggled over onto his belly, turned his head, shook his tail. He gathered his legs under himself and—"Oh no!"

"What is it?" Toaff came closer.

Without looking, the little squirrel said, "My front—" Then he turned and saw who had spoken. He tried to back away, but one of his front legs didn't want to touch the ground. The wild eyes stared at Toaff and he asked, "How do you do it? Because I fell, didn't I? I remember falling. But I *can* jump, I've done it. Not like you, but— And now my leg isn't—" He rose onto three legs, and held the fourth up above the ground. "I can't—" He sank down again. "I guess I'm done for."

Toaff didn't argue. If a squirrel couldn't climb or run, there wasn't much hope for him.

"Anyway," the little animal announced almost cheerfully, "it's still cold enough that maybe I'll have frozen to death before a fox finds me."

That *fox* decided Toaff. "Can you walk? Nilf, that's your name, isn't it? Can you walk on your other legs?"

"How do you know my name? Have you been spying on us?"

"Of course not. Those others said it. *Can* you walk?"

"Probably. Maybe. Maybe sort of, probably. But I can't run. Or climb."

"Then walk," Toaff urged. *Fox, fox, fox* echoed around in his head.

Nilf took a step, and stumbled up against Toaff. "It *hurts*. It's *hard* to—" He held out his injured front leg. "I don't think I— Stop staring! You're— What's your name, can you go away now?"

"Toaff," Toaff answered, and took a deep breath, to help himself stay patient. "If you leaned on me, could you walk?"

"I can't climb," Nilf pointed out.

"My den doesn't have to be climbed into."

"You think I'm going to *your* den?"

"I could take you to yours," Toaff offered.

"They'd eat you alive," Nilf said, and explained, "They hate you."

"Then we'll go to mine," Toaff said patiently. "But we have to get moving."

"I can't," Nilf said. "It's—it's too far!"

"If you stay here, you're foxfood," Toaff argued.

"I don't want to—"

"You don't have a choice," Toaff argued.

"—not with a Chukchuk, it's—"

"I can't fight off a fox," Toaff pointed out.

42

"—not safe," Nilf insisted.

Toaff didn't want to stand around quarreling. A moving squirrel had a chance. A squirrel standing around quarreling was asking to be someone's dinner. "You're coming with me," he said. "You have to," he announced.

"No I don't," Nilf argued. "And I can't."

Toaff got behind him and pushed. "Move," he ordered. "You have to help me."

"I don't *want* to go with you!" Nilf said, and he tried to squirm aside. "I can't! I'll fall!" But Toaff kept on shoving and pushing. Finally, taking a lesson from Braff, he nipped the smaller squirrel, on his rump.

"Hey!" Nilf protested. "That was—!"

"You *have* to try."

"All right," Nilf said. "All right, I will. Just don't bite me again."

# A GUEST WHO
# WANTS TO LEAVE

Because Nilf had to lean against Toaff to walk, they moved in a mostly forward but partly sideways direction through the woods to the drive. Once there, they sheltered briefly under a pine. Toaff checked up the drive to the red nest and the white nest-house, then in the other direction, where the road lay. No machine was moving. He listened carefully, but heard no distant rumbling, so they went lurching slowly and clumsily across the dirt. That danger safely past, Toaff moved behind Nilf, to push him forward through the field to the broken pine.

But it felt like the closer they got to his tree, the harder it was to push the little Churrchurr along. If he hadn't known better, Toaff would have thought Nilf was pushing backward, trying not to be rescued. He couldn't *not* want to be rescued, could he?

The leg did have to hurt, though, because at each step, Nilf gave a little muffled whimper. So Toaff didn't try to rush him, and he didn't complain about how clumsy and slow their progress was. He kept moving, all of his senses alert for danger, heading home.

The last part of the long journey was the most difficult for both of them. As they went up the slanting trunk of the broken pine, Toaff shoved at the small red rump and tried not to trip over, or be blinded by, the feathery tail. It didn't help that Nilf seemed to be digging his claws into the wood to resist each step. It felt as if Nilf was trying to back down, not climb up. But that was so nonsensical, Toaff decided it couldn't be true, and just kept pushing until at last he could shove Nilf up through the entrance. With a squeal of pain, his guest tumbled into the den.

In the dim light of late afternoon inside the dead pine, Toaff watched the dark shape feel its way around until it found the soft nest. There it settled, sitting up on its haunches. Not until then did Toaff follow, asking, "Are you hungr—?"

The little Churrchurr turned on him, teeth bared, snarling.

Snarling? Was he as crazy as his eyes? "What is it now?" Toaff demanded.

"Stay back," Nilf snarled.

"This is *my* den," Toaff pointed out.

He might as well not have spoken.

"I may be injured and you may have been able to force me to come here, but I've still got teeth," Nilf warned.

"Are you afraid of me?"

The answer came too quickly. "Afraid? No. Not one bit."

"Hunhh," Toaff said.

Then, "*Should* I be afraid of you?" Nilf wondered.

"You're acting afraid," Toaff explained. He knew what fear smelled like and it was definitely fear he was smelling, coming off the little animal.

"Whyever would I be frightened?" Nilf asked. "Except that you're twice my size and a Gray. One of the big fat gray Chukchuks who keep trying to take over our territory."

This Churrchurr was one surprise after another. "Why would I want your territory?"

Nilf didn't have to stop and think. This was something he had always known. "Because you hate us. Also, you want our stores." At least, talking seemed to calm him a little.

"I've got plenty of stores of my own. Right here," Toaff pointed out. "Why would I want yours?"

Again, it was as if he hadn't spoken. Nilf went right on. "All we have is our one little territory but that's good enough for us. We don't try to take more. You Grays can go anywhere you like, no matter how far off, miles and miles, everybody says, everybody knows. But you still want to take ours away from us."

Why would Nilf lie to him? Toaff asked himself. No reason, he answered. But Toaff had never heard anything about gray squirrels wanting to move across the drive into the Churrchurrs' territory, so "How do you know that?" he wondered.

"Everybody says," Nilf answered.

By then the Churrchurr no longer smelled of fear. Toaff took two steps closer and asked again, "Aren't you hungry?"

46

"Maybe." The answer came slowly, almost reluctantly. "Maybe not." Nilf backed away from Toaff, backing deeper into the nest.

"Is that why they all chased after me?" Toaff asked.

"What do you Chukchuks expect us to do?" Nilf answered.

There was a long silence. Finally Nilf took a deep breath and said, "You know, if you're going to kill me and eat me? I'd rather you just did it."

"Kill you? Eat you? Is that what you think? You *do* realize that if I wanted you dead, I'd have left you for a fox, don't you? And spared myself the work of getting you up here. Think about that, Nilf," Toaff said, and he was angry now. "Anyway, *I'm* hungry and *I'm* going to have a chestnut because—frankly?—I suspect that squirrel tastes disgusting. There's a chestnut for you, too, if you want some."

"How do I know it's not gone rotten? And gotten poisonous?"

Toaff had had enough of this from the little Churrchurr, whose life he might, after all, have just saved. "You *should* be worried, because of course I keep a special supply of rotten chestnuts, in case there is some Churrchurr"—and Toaff rattled off the next words quickly—"who has fallen out of his *own* trees in his *own* woods across the drive, where, by the way, it's dangerous for me to go, and been abandoned by his *own* friends, and I can push him across the open all the way back to my den so that, if we don't get eaten on the way, I can poison him once we're here. It's the kind of thing that happens all the time. That's why I need to keep a supply of rotten chestnuts handy."

Nilf was silent for a long time. At last, very quietly, he asked, "How can I tell?"

"If you don't want to stay, you're welcome to leave," Toaff told him.

"You know I can't."

Toaff didn't say anything to that. He just went over to where his stores lay in a pile. Braff was right to warn him; his supplies *were* dwindling. Still, he carried a chestnut over to Nilf before he took his own out to the entrance. There, he sat up on his haunches and gnawed crossly, looking at the pasture and the sky. He didn't like all this quarreling. He'd rather wrestle and whuffle any day.

Darkness drifted down out of the sky, spreading over the pasture and trees and the distant nest-house. In the morning, Toaff knew, Nilf would either be fine or he would be dead. That was the way with squirrels, they either died or healed, and it didn't take long. Although if Nilf was going to die in Toaff's den, Toaff would have to move out. Watching the slowly darkening pasture, he thought of the apple trees, which had been able to withstand the winter storm. He went back inside, considering what to do about the stores if Nilf died.

The Churrchurr was already asleep, but as soon as Toaff got into the nest, he woke up. "Get away! I can bite even if I can't run."

"It's just me," Toaff said. So much fierceness from such

a scrawny little squirrel was ridiculous. "And it's my own nest, if you remember." He couldn't stop himself from whuffling.

"What do you mean, *just* you?" Nilf demanded, but he had started to whuffle, too. "You're too big to be *just* anything," he pointed out. "And fat," he added, then whuffled uncontrollably.

"Oh . . . just . . . go back to sleep," Toaff said, trying to sound bored and impatient but actually feeling a lot better now, about everything. When you whuffled at the same things, did other differences matter?

# LEAPING LESSONS

Toaff was relieved to see that what awaited him in the morning was not the stiff body of a dead squirrel, but a bright-eyed, hungry Churrchurr, impatient to know "Will you? Will you show me how to leap? Like you do?"

Of course Toaff agreed. How could he not like being admired? They ate quickly, then Toaff led the little squirrel across to the horse chestnut tree.

"We're better runners," Nilf told him. "Chukchuks aren't nearly as fast, everybody says."

"I got here first, didn't I?"

"But you never said where we were going so I *had* to follow you. Anyway, it's easy to see why you're slower," Nilf said. "You lope, like a rabbit. You push off with your back paws together and land with your front paws together. *Calumph-calumph, calumph-calumph.* I'm not saying you're slow, you're just not . . . We use our legs one after the other, *da-da-da-da, da-da-da-da.* That's what makes us faster."

Toaff tried running that way and it felt wrong. He practically stumbled, so he pretended he didn't care. He had climbed up the chestnut trunk and then out onto a high branch before he looked back.

The little red squirrel had stopped moving back where the branch began and sat huddled up as close to the trunk as he could get.

Toaff ran back to where the little red squirrel crouched with all eighteen of his nails digging in. "What's wrong?"

"I—" Nilf began, but stopped to gulp in air. His wild eyes stared at Toaff and his voice got tiny. "It's so high. Higher than my pines, and in my pines there are all these wide branches underneath. But this . . ."

Toaff looked down and he saw, for the first time, how very far below the branches the ground was and how very narrow the bare branch ahead. "I *know* it's safe," he said. "Really."

Nilf shook his head.

Toaff pointed out, "It's safer when the branches are bare like this because you can see everything, and that means you can see which are the good branches. That's why you fell, you know. You couldn't see to choose a good branch."

"Don't make me think about falling," Nilf said.

Toaff remembered how the little red body had gone tumbling through branches. "You don't have to do this," he said.

"But I want to!" Nilf cried.

"Why?" Toaff asked. But he thought he knew. *Afraid* was a helpless, hopeless word, the mouse in the fox's jaws.

*Afraid* was a word that went on too long before it ended, sharp as a shriek.

"So I can cross the drive without a machine squishing me," Nilf answered.

"Why do you want to cross the drive?"

"So I can see if there's a holly bush in those woods beyond your pasture."

"What difference would a holly bush make?" Toaff asked, but Nilf—again!—wasn't listening.

"And I *want* to, too, because you must feel like a bird when *you* do it. So let's get going," Nilf decided.

He was certainly brave enough, Toaff thought as he led the little squirrel out to the end of the branch. There, he pointed out a branch on the first maple. "See it? And you want to land close enough to the trunk that the branch doesn't sink under you."

"I'm not nearly as big and fat as you," Nilf said.

"You're big enough," Toaff promised him. "And if the branch sways down, and you can't get a grip? You've already fallen once," he reminded the red squirrel.

"Unnhh," Nilf said, and said no more, so Toaff thought that he had probably won *that* argument, at least. He knew he was right, too. About leaping, Toaff already knew a lot.

"Watch," he said. He gathered his legs under him and leaped out.

It wasn't much of a leap. Having landed easily on the branch he'd shown Nilf, Toaff ran up to another, from which to return with a longer, more satisfying leap. Back on the chestnut, he climbed down to where Nilf waited. "Now you," he said. "You do it."

And Nilf did.

Toaff believed that the little Churrchurr really was afraid and so, although it wasn't a great distance and the landing was clumsy, Toaff was sincerely impressed. "Perfect!" he called, and jumped over to join Nilf.

"It won't be so easy when these trees grow leaves," Nilf warned. "I came outside last spring and I've seen them."

"There are no leaves now," Toaff pointed out. "Do you want me to go next?"

"No," Nilf decided. He took a deep breath. "I will."

When he stood behind the little squirrel and watched, Toaff saw why Churrchurrs didn't jump well. Nilf used one leg after the other to push off, *da-da-da-da*, just as he did for running along the ground. Toaff used both of his back legs, together, *push*. He tried to explain this as they continued practicing, going across and back, from the maple to the chestnut back to the maple, over and over. But Nilf couldn't seem to do it.

"My legs don't work that way," he concluded, and because Toaff had been unable to run like a Churrchurr himself, Toaff didn't argue. "The more you practice, the better you'll be" was all he said.

Nilf practiced until he was breathless with the constant overcoming of fear and the jumping; then he sat down on the chestnut branch and said, "Home."

Toaff led him back toward the broken pine.

"Aren't you hungry?" he asked, because by then he certainly was.

"I meant *my* home," Nilf said. "But I wouldn't mind eating first."

Not much later, they sat on the broken branch below the entrance in the warmth of a midday sun, chewing. "Winter's going," Nilf observed. "Aren't you glad?"

"Winter's beautiful," Toaff said. He remembered the bare branches black against the snow. "And it's exciting," he added, thinking of winds fierce enough to break a pine in half. "And I've got stores. Enough, I think."

"Enough for you and whoever it is you're sharing them with?"

Toaff turned to stare at this odd little squirrel, with his pointy ears and wild eyes. "What do you mean, sharing? I'm not sharing. There's just me."

"I mean there was less in your pile of stores when we came back than there was when we went out. Didn't you notice? So someone must have taken some." Nilf glanced briefly at Toaff.

"I've got enough stores," Toaff said again.

Nilf told him, "No squirrel has enough stores unless he lives in the nest-barn."

"What's the nest-barn?"

"It's the big red nest," Nilf told him.

"Oh." A nest-barn? How many nests did humans need? "Do squirrels live there?" Toaff asked.

"Not anymore but some used to. They always had

54

plenty of food because of the cows. The humans feed the cows. You could stay inside all winter long if you wanted and it was always warm."

Cows? Toaff wondered, but he had a more important question. "Why *used to*?"

"Cats," Nilf said. "Two of them. Those nest-barn cats will hunt you down to eat and sometimes they hunt you down just to kill you. It was too dangerous."

"Do you know of anywhere really safe?" Toaff asked.

"Not for a squirrel. Maybe for dogs and cats and humans there's somewhere. It's saf*er* where hollies are, that's all I know. But nothing's *really* safe."

"My den is safe," Toaff said. He wondered if the little Churrchurr might come back sometime. Grays and Churrchurrs might hate each other, but he and Nilf didn't, did they?

"I have to go," Nilf said. "It's beginning to feel wrong." While they had been eating, the little squirrel had become more and more uneasy. He looked up and around, and he looked down and around. His paws danced on the stump. Now his tail curled over his back as if to protect him, now he held it out low and stiff. Nilf was so nervous, he was making Toaff nervous, too. "I'm going," Nilf said, and without another word or a backward glance, he skittered down the pine trunk and ran—really fast—across to the chestnut to jump over to the first maple and then to the next and the next, before he leaped across the drive and disappeared into his own woods.

Toaff sighed, and went inside to look at his stores.

# TOAFF THE DEFENDER

After Nilf, there was wind. Day after day, the wind blew, strong and ceaseless. This was a roaring wind that pulled at the branches of the two firs. This was a rough wind that tore winter-weakened limbs from the maples as it raged by. Sometimes the wind spat out fat, wet flakes of snow. More often it pounded rain down against the fields and trees. Gradually, rain melted away the last patches of snow as, just as gradually, the wind blew itself out.

Toaff spent those stormy days and nights snug in his den. Not until it was quiet again did he venture out, to forage. At the entrance, he hesitated, dismayed. The scattered limbs didn't surprise him, but he was shocked at what he saw in the woods beyond the pasture. Roots were clutching at the air, with clumps of dirt still wrapped about them. How could it be that a tree's long roots were torn up out of the earth that held them safe?

It was because Toaff was hesitating that he saw Braff's slow, silent approach from behind the horse chestnut. If he had been out foraging, as usual, he never would have known. But he *was* there and he *did* know so he chukked loudly, "Go away!"

Braff ran up to the tip of the pine and stopped there. He looked up at Toaff and flicked his tail. "What do you mean, go away?"

"The stores are mine." Toaff stepped out onto the broken branch and flicked his own tail, in warning.

"They're mine as much as yours," Braff announced.

"Not anymore," Toaff told him.

They stared at one another, both fat silver tails flicking fast.

Braff said, "I know something you don't."

Toaff kept quiet. What were you supposed to answer when someone said that?

"If I told you what I know, you'd be really sorry you stayed here."

It wasn't easy not to ask Braff what he was talking about.

"Or maybe I'll come back—but not alone."

With that, Braff turned away. After a couple of steps he looked back at Toaff to announce, "It's something else the rabbits said. They were outside last spring, they told us what happens. The human doesn't like branches in the drive and he won't like this broken tree either, right in his pasture. There's something bad he's going to do to it and then what will you eat? With all your stores gone. Where will you live?"

Toaff didn't stop to think. "In the apple trees."

Braff whuffled. "How? In a drey? Have you noticed how

*short* an apple tree is? Your drey would hang down to the ground." He whuffled some more. "You'll have to think of something better than that, Toaff."

Braff started off again, but stopped again, to call, "And you better think fast. That's all I'm going to tell you." He was almost at the horse chestnut before he turned back a third time. "It's called a chain saw," he chukked, but before Toaff could ask what he was talking about, Braff said, "We're going to cross the road into a new woods where there won't be Churrchurrs, to start up their stealing. You can come."

"Don't you remember how dangerous the road is?" Toaff asked. "They warned us, don't you remember? The road is much more dangerous than the drive."

"You only have to make it across once," Braff answered. "Are you going to come with us? Or not."

Toaff didn't have to think about that either. "Not," he answered, and Braff started off again. This time he ran across to the nearest maple without turning around, and ran up its trunk.

Toaff raced down to the ground and over to the chestnut. He scurried up it and out onto a branch to be sure Braff really was leaving and not trying a trick to lure Toaff away. He waited there long after Braff was out of sight, on his guard, being proud of the way he'd defended his stores.

That was when he saw the fox. Maybe it was the same fox, maybe another. All foxes looked alike. The fox was on the hunt, of course.

It moved slowly, nose to the ground. Its paws landed delicately, so gently that the damp mounds of brown grass showed no trace of its passing, as it patiently tracked its prey. The prey, a creature small enough to hide under the grass, kept to the edge of the pasture, hoping to shelter among the stones of the wall that separated the pasture from the pale new grass growing by the drive. That prey must be desperately hungry, Toaff thought, to come foraging in the open, in daylight.

Toaff wanted to run to the opposite side of the chestnut and not see what was going to happen. He wanted to run back into his den and not hear anything. He couldn't stand to watch another mouse caught in a fox's jaws. He couldn't stand to hear another shriek. He wished he was a dog, big enough to fight a fox, or a raptor with claws to stick into a fox's rump. A squirrel couldn't attack a fox. Squirrels weren't fighters. They were quarrelers, who used voices to attack, not claws and teeth.

*What if I—?*

Toaff took off into empty air, mouth wide open, and his high-pitched, sharp-edged cry flew with him. *Screetteeettee! Screetteeettee!* He didn't dare look at the fox or try to see the mouse. He had to keep his eyes fixed on the thin chestnut branch below him and then, when he landed, he needed to concentrate all of his attention on keeping his balance, keeping his sharp nails dug into the new, soft bark—*Screetteeettee!* he cried, *Screetteeettee!* again, and again—as the branch swayed down toward the ground,

59

closer to the fox, then rose up before it sank down again. *Screetteeettee!*

When he *could* look, Toaff saw the fox with its ears cocked, turning in one direction after another as it tried to locate the lost prey. The fox stuck its nose into one mound of grass, then another. Keeping an eye on the fox, Toaff scampered back up along the low, swaying branch, and when he'd reached the safe place where it joined the trunk, he stopped, sat up on his haunches with his paws gathered into his chest, his tail high and proud behind him, and whuffled. He felt ready for anything.

He had never heard of any other squirrel attacking a fox. He was the only one.

# SPRING

# BRAFF'S FAREWELL

Then the sun-filled air had no edge of cold to it, and the smallest of breezes blew warmth across the pasture. Rains fell as gentle as sunlight and even the *kaah-kaah*s of crows sounded softer. The air smelled of promises, but of what Toaff couldn't know. All he knew was that winter was over. Quiet as snowfall, spring had slipped into the farm.

With spring came a distant, ugly noise, a whining machine noise, unlike anything Toaff had ever heard. This machine didn't move along the drive the way machines usually did. His ears told him that this machine stayed in one place, although that place changed from day to day. Another difference was the way it started up and after not very long fell silent, waited, then started up again, sometimes right away, sometimes after a long delay. It was a stop-and-start, standing-still machine, and Toaff had no idea what that kind of machine might look like, or what it might do to a squirrel. But the thing kept its distance so he didn't worry.

What he did worry about in those early-spring days was Braff. Toaff no longer had enough stores to share. He kept close to home those days, and on the lookout. Thus it was that one spring morning, when he glimpsed six gray shapes skittering across the pasture toward his pine, he made sure he got to the entrance first. He didn't have to look twice to recognize the squirrel in the lead, but the other five he hadn't seen before.

Toaff made his stand on the broken branch by his entrance, his tail held high and straight. He flicked it, warning those squirrels off, threatening them. At the same time he chukked loudly, "Stop!! Get away!" Then he thought to add, "I'll bite!" even though he didn't know if he actually would bite, or if he even *could*. In his experience, squirrels were threateners, not fighters. They chuk-chukked until one or the other backed off. Why one or the other backed off was not clear. Some fierceness in the enemy that was greater than the fierceness he felt in himself, maybe. Or maybe, one squirrel wasn't quite as hungry as the other?

Braff halted halfway up the pine trunk and the others halted behind him. Toaff waited. These were *his* stores.

Braff whuffled. "Take it easy, Toaff. We're just here to give you a chance to come with us. Oh, and warn you."

"Warn me about what?"

"You hear that machine?" Braff asked.

Toaff didn't answer. Of course he heard it. He'd been hearing it for days. What kind of a question was that?

"That's a chain saw machine. The human uses it to cut fallen trees into pieces, if they fell near the drive. He also uses it on any big branches that blew down. They"—he gave a nod of his head toward the line of squirrels behind him—"used to live on the other side of the white nest and they know all about the chain saw machine. After a storm, the human cuts up fallen trees and big branches."

"This tree isn't near the drive," Toaff pointed out.

"The human doesn't like fallen things," Braff insisted. "He cuts them up with his chain saw machine. Which you can hear right now. That's one of the reasons we're going across the road where there's nothing but woods. No humans, Toaff, and that means no cats and no dogs and no machines either. You can come, too," he offered again.

Toaff said, "The road has a lot more machines than the drive. Everyone says. A really lot more."

"I'm not afraid," Braff answered. He turned to ask of his followers, "You fellows afraid?"

"Not me" and "Nossir" and "Not a bit," they answered.

"What about you, Toaff?" Braff asked. "Are you afraid?"

Toaff didn't answer. Of course he was, but why say it?

"So, are you coming with us? Or not?" Braff asked again, and "Not," Toaff answered again. He kept on blocking the entrance, in case this was some trick.

Braff waited, and waited a little more, until at last he asked, "Are you going to at least give us something to eat before we go?"

Toaff didn't say anything.

"All right," Braff said. "Have it your way. Too bad for you, Toaff." He waited some more but Toaff neither moved nor spoke, so Braff turned to his companions to give the order: "Let's get going!"

"Good luck!" Toaff called to him, watching the line of squirrels run lightly back down the pine, watching them cross in a line to a maple, tails raised high and eager, then climb any which way up into its branches. "Good luck!" he called again, and he really did mean it.

For a long time Toaff watched the trees into which the squirrels had disappeared. He watched until the air grew too dark to see anything but shadows. Then he went into his den, where he curled up in his nest, wrapped his tail around himself, and fell into a warm, dark sleep.

# EVERYTHING CHANGES, AGAIN

A whole field of mice shrieked, shrieked without stopping, shrieked and shrieked and shrieked. Screeching crows flew up into the air and circled there, screeching. Shrieking and screeching: The high-pitched sounds that were pouring into the den squeezed out all the air.

Terror made Toaff stupid. He jumped back, to the wall farthest from the entrance—even though it wasn't very far at all and certainly not far enough to escape the noise. He couldn't hear. He couldn't see. He smelled wood, and it smelled hot. Wood shouldn't smell hot, and there was something thick and black and nasty, too.

*Run! Run!* terror whispered into his ears, sliding its voice in under the shrieks and screeches.

But Toaff was in his den and the noise was just beyond his entrance. He would run right into its jaws.

Or talons— Right into its hard, sharp talons.

Toaff backed up as close as he could get to the wall, sat up on his haunches, and stared at the round, bright entrance. He struggled for breath.

Suddenly, silence. Silence fell down hard, and it was

as loud as the shrieking. His ears rang with the silence and still his breath came in gulps but now fear pushed him away from the wall with its same message: *Run! Run! Get out!*

Toaff could no more have hesitated than he could have tunneled his way down through the long trunk to safety. He certainly didn't take time to think, to wonder what he'd find, what he'd see, what might be waiting out there. He burst through the entrance.

What waited was something large, and alive, and bent over a big horse chestnut branch blown off by winter storms. Except the branch wasn't big anymore, and the large living thing straightened up. It was tall. It had an orange head. And it was coming toward Toaff's broken pine.

He fled. He skittered down to the tip of the pine, and hovered behind it, waiting, trying to think. Did he dare try to reach the horse chestnut? Was it safer to stay where he was? Was this a hunter, just waiting for him to appear in the open?

His heart pounded and he could not slow the frantic waving of his tail, but he was now outside, where a squirrel had room to run—run across, run up, run away—and squirrels could outrun most predators on the ground, for a little while at least. He took a brief look at the something-large.

It was a human, by the shape of it, a giant figure with a huge round head that now moved from the horse chestnut right up to Toaff's broken pine. It lifted its front legs, and as soon as it did that, the terrible shrieks began again.

This noise had to be a machine. What had Braff called

it? A chain saw machine? The chestnut tree was, for a squirrel, at this moment, the only safe place.

Toaff ran.

He scrambled across the stone wall and up the horse chestnut. Safely there, Toaff squeezed his eyes shut and crouched close to the trunk, nails digging deep into the branch. He heard the high shrieks and then a heavy thump and a silence, then more shrieks and thumps, then another silence. Even with his eyes closed, he couldn't think of anything to do next. He reminded himself that he was on a branch low enough that a squirrel could jump from it down to the ground and maybe not smash himself to death and maybe have a chance to run, although probably not. Eyes shut, head down, Toaff huddled and hoped and had to hear.

Eventually the sound stopped. The loud silence that it left behind faded away into the usual daily noises of the farm, into insect conversations and bird words. A breeze whispered through the two firs. Toaff could even hear the dogs, who now came bounding up to the human, both of them jabbering away at the same time. Toaff understood very little of what they said and the little he understood had no meaning for him. "*Yark* gone, *yark*," Angus said, and "*Yarkyark* loud," Sadie said.

One reason Toaff didn't understand was because both dogs were talking at the same time. Another was that he had opened his eyes. With his eyes open, he could see the empty space where his broken pine had been. A stump was all that remained there, a stump with a pile of wood chunks beside it. There was no broken-off tree trunk jabbing splintered wood up into the air. There was no long section of tree resting its tip on the ground. Especially, there was no hollow den where a nest and stores waited for Toaff when he returned.

There were no stores, and even if there had been, there was no place for Toaff to pile them up in. There was no nest where he could sleep. There was nothing left for him.

# APPLE TREES

Toaff crept down the thick horse chestnut trunk, watching out for the dogs but not too worried. The dogs were busy snuffling at the pieces of the dead pine, which the human was making into a pile. Did humans have stores of tree pieces? Did that mean that humans ate trees?

The dogs yarked and snuffled at the same time: "Smell that?" "No, what?" "Furry meaty—" "*Yark* nothing, Sadie." "I *do*, I smell squirrel!" "No you don't." "But Angus—"

Toaff ran to the stone wall and scrambled up to the top to see any possible danger, either from the dogs in the pasture behind him or the humans from the nest-house ahead. He stuck his nose down into the cracks between the stones to be sure he could squeeze into them, if he had to, then continued on along the top of the wall, crouching low, looking up for possible danger from overhead. He was heading for the apple trees, and their apples.

The two apple trees grew close together. The first had a slim trunk that rose straight out of the ground, with no roots showing. The second had more branches and looked older, a little bent over, rounder and sturdier. Its roots spread out a little before they dug down into the earth. But the younger tree was taller and Toaff saw a nest resting on one of its bare branches, so that was the one he chose.

When he had climbed up to it, he could see how the nest had been tucked in close against the smooth trunk. It was made of twigs and dried grass and smelled faintly of whatever bird had lived in it. Toaff reasoned that this nest had survived the storms of winter and the winds of early spring, so it must be safe. Besides, a single black crow's feather waited there, as if to say, *This is a good place.* He jumped down into the nest and sat there, getting used to it.

In the afternoon Toaff climbed down to forage around the trunks of the two trees, and found no sign of even the one apple he'd left buried in the snow there. He went back to search along the edge of the stone wall. It took a while but he found enough to fill his stomach. As the sun's light was fading, he returned to the nest and fell quickly asleep.

Until rain woke him.

There was no light. Cold drops of water fell out of the darkness onto Toaff's head and shoulders and rump and he curled his tail more tightly around himself, trying not to wake up. But he was awake. And wet. What did birds do, out in the open like this, with just their feathers to protect them? Why

didn't birds have dens? For that matter, why didn't Toaff have a den, to keep him dry and warm? In the darkness and alone, as a cold rain fell on him, Toaff wished: He wished the human hadn't come around with his chain saw machine. He wished he'd gone with Braff and the others, even if it meant he had to cross the road, even if it meant being whuffled at and bossed around. He wished hardest that the dead pine hadn't been cracked in half and blown over and changed everything. As the black night dragged itself along and the cold rain fell down, Toaff almost wished that he hadn't been able to save himself from that machine on the drive, all that time ago.

And that— Was it common sense that made room for this idea? Or was it the first gray light of day spreading up into the falling rain that was almost enough to make a miserable little squirrel whuffle? Any squirrel knew it was better to be alive than dead. But it kept raining, all morning, and Toaff couldn't make himself leave the sodden nest. He was tired, he was hungry, he was wet and cold, and he didn't want to move. Why should he move from one wet place to another? What else could he do but wait, and wait, and wait still longer?

He hadn't known he could be so uncomfortable.

When the rain at last stopped, Toaff scurried down to the ground and over to the stone wall. Then, as if it had been waiting for the rain to get out of its way, the sun appeared, to warm Toaff's fur and the stones under his paws. He found no more than a few dried seeds, but he was hungry enough to be happy with that. He sat on the wall, chewing hard. He looked at the branches beyond the top of the nest-house. He wondered what he should do, and he tried not to remember the piles of stores he'd lost, and he couldn't forget them. But this caused him to think about his crowded den, with so many squirrels chuk-chukking together, and telling stories and warning one another, and this led him to finally remember something useful: He remembered a voice making fun of Churrchurrs because they lived in burrows.

In burrows dug in the ground! Burrows dug in the ground among the roots of trees!

Toaff scrambled back over the rocks to the older apple tree, to study its roots. Looking carefully, he could see a place where two fat roots joined the trunk, leaving a little hollow on the ground between them. Toaff set right to work, digging at damp dirt to make it deeper, then gathering dry grass to pile up in it, to make a nest where a squirrel could sleep. That night, if it rained, he would be protected. That night he would be able to sleep.

What Toaff didn't understand until it was too late was that he didn't have an actual burrow. An actual burrow is an underground den. What he had was a nest half sunk into the ground among a tree's roots. He might as well have been trying to sleep out in the middle of a field. What kept Toaff awake that second night was not rain. It was waiting for some fox or cat or raccoon to spring at him from out of the darkness, and sink its sharp teeth into him.

As soon as it was light, Toaff fled to the top of the tree. He hoped that from its branches he might see something, anything, useful. But there was just the nest he had already tried and his own little hollow. Neither one of these was a place where a squirrel wanted to live. Toaff had no place to sleep. *And* it had started to rain, again. *And* he was hungry. He decided he'd have to find those trees on the other side of the nest-house. But first, he *had* to eat.

A few small buds, fed by rain and encouraged by sun, had come out at the very tips of the twigs at the narrowest ends of this tree's thinnest branches. It was dangerous to try for them, but what choice did he have? He was weak with both hunger and sleeplessness. That was no way to start off on a trek. Slowly, cautiously, Toaff edged out along a branch. There—softly, gently—he gathered one bud, two, barely moving at all to reach them, then three and four, holding them all in his mouth. They were hard and bitter, but they were food. It was risky to turn around but it was even riskier to back up. So, with the most delicate movements of which a squirrel is capable, as if trying not to disturb the air around him, Toaff rotated.

That was when he saw it. Just below where he was balanced, at the end of a short fat stump where a branch must have been torn off, Toaff saw a round hole that maybe was an entrance. This was so surprising and welcome a sight that he almost slipped from his perch. He almost spat out the buds he had just gathered, and at such risk. As carefully as he had made his way out, he made his way back to the trunk. He chewed and swallowed hastily, tasting nothing of what was in his mouth, then he went to take a look.

Because if there was a hollow, it had to be unoccupied, otherwise he would have seen some other squirrel. Because if there was any kind of a hollow, he could make it large enough to hold a nest that would be out of the rain and hidden from predators. Because he might have found a safe place.

# EARLY SPRING

Early spring was just as bad as everyone had said. Toaff went to bed hungry and stayed hungry all during nights that seemed endless. He woke up hungry and wished he could go back to sleep. He had to forage long and hard just to find enough food to give him the strength to go out foraging when he woke up hungry the next morning.

Early spring was rainy days and weak sunlight, fog that kept you in your nest for fear of hidden predators, followed by long dark nights trapped in your den with your hunger and your bad thoughts. Nothing felt right in early spring, and it went on and on and on, day after day after day, until Toaff almost couldn't remember what winter had been like, in a big den with piles of stores nearby.

Then came a morning when everything—sky and trees, even the dirt drive and even the black crow that soared over the nest-house, *kaah-kaah*ing—everything was as bright as if the whole farm was newly made. The nest-house shone bright white and every pine and fir shone too, shone dark green. The grass shone pale green, while the patches of bare earth out of which it was grown shone brown. The air tasted of never-before-seen things. Toaff breathed in that air, and looked across the top of the nest-house to those high branches. *What if I—?*

But the roaring and grinding of a machine started up. The machine was in the pasture where his pine had stood, which was too close. He decided to stay where he was. All that day the machine roared and all day long Toaff sat trembling on an apple branch, hoping that nothing terrible was about to happen.

The machine was carrying the human and dragging behind it a wide dark path of fresh dirt, dragging dirt back and forth, until the whole pasture was changed. Then the machine went away. When it had gone, some crows called, *Kaah-kaah*. What might they be saying? Could they be speaking to him? They flew down to hop around on the dark surface and sometimes dart their beaks down into the dirt, and took off again, *Kaah-kaah*. Saying, *Your turn* or maybe *Food here!* Toaff went to find out.

In the pasture, bugs squirmed up and down through the new dirt, peeking out, crawling in. Hungry as he was, he wasn't hungry enough to eat a bug, but lots of old, flavorless seeds poked out of the dirt. Those Toaff did eat, until his stomach was finally full and he could return to the safety of his nest, to not be hungry all night and to make plans. He didn't want to stay in the apple tree any longer.

But that was the night he first heard a new, and strange, voice. The voice came out of the big white nest-house. This was a long voice that ran along without stopping, like a squirrel on a branch. It was a slender sound that swayed gently down and then floated up into the air. It was curved and silvery, like the tail of a squirrel. The sound wound around him. He couldn't imagine what name such a sound might have. For as long as it went on, Toaff lay with his nose resting on the entryway to his tiny den and listened, and listened, until it stopped and was gone.

The sound had come from the nest-house. So was it human? But when the human talked to the dogs, his voice didn't sound like this. But if it wasn't human, what else could it be? Could a creature make sounds so very different from its usual voice? That would be like Toaff being able to *kaah* like a crow, which he definitely couldn't, or yark. But humans weren't like other animals, as Toaff already knew.

This was made even clearer to him the very next morning. As he was squeezing out of his nest, he heard the crows calling. They could have been telling him to *Look, look!* so he did, and saw a new human, who stood on a low pile of wood sticking out from the front of the nest-house. This human was different from the man—a female? A mate? Her front legs waved in the air, graceful as a squirrel's tail, and white things flew out of them, scattering down onto the ground. The crows flew up, *kaah-kaah*ing, to drive her back. When she was gone, they landed in the grass and hopped about, stabbing at the ground with their beaks, eating. Eating what? Toaff sat on a branch, wondering, watching, and after not very long, the crows flew off.

*What if I—?*

He scrambled down the trunk and dashed across to that part of the grass where the crows had been. He was too hungry to be as careful as he should have, but nothing unlucky happened and his curiosity was rewarded by pale chunks of something that smelled like food lying among the blades of grass. He took a bite and it was good, although not at all in the way a nut or seed was good, and it was much softer even than a horse chestnut. He gobbled one down quickly, then a second, and then, finally noticing how unprotected he was, he picked up another of the squares in his teeth, to carry it up close to the nest-house. In that protected place, he sat on his haunches to enjoy eating.

He was enjoying it slowly, chewing, tasting, swallowing, enjoying it a lot, when two things happened in quick succession and he forgot about food:

First, he saw a flash of movement on the far side of the big white nest-house. Was it a gray squirrel? Before he could be sure, he was distracted by more movement on that same side of the nest-house, and this was the slow, low movement of a hunt.

Toaff may have never before in his life seen a cat, but he knew these two were cats. So did the watching crows, who *kaah-kaah*ed an alarm from the air. The might-be-a-squirrel disappeared. The cats bounded after.

Toaff fled back to the apple tree.

By the time he was safely perched on a branch, the grass was empty and the nest-house quiet, all of its many entrances dark. No crows hovered in the sky. The cats were gone. Toaff guessed that if it *was* a squirrel he'd seen, it must live in those trees on the far side of the nest-house. He guessed that squirrel might also have been looking for food, and that made him notice how full his stomach was. That made him think how good it was not to be hungry, and that made him wonder if he could hope that early spring was over.

# SPRING SURPRISES

Not many days later, Toaff stuck his head out into bright morning air and believed—for five amazed breaths, or ten—that in the night he had been carried up into the sky. Tiny puffy white clouds had appeared all around him— beneath him, beside him, and above him, too—and the air smelled entirely different. The air smelled wonderful! He had no name for what the air smelled of, but he figured out soon enough that it wasn't clouds around him. It was some new part of the apple tree. His apple tree was filled with little white bursts, not as white as snow but thick as snow could be, and they were the source of that wonderful smell.

Toaff sniffed and sniffed and whuffled to himself.

He wasn't surprised when Sadie and Angus and even the mate came to admire what the apple tree had done. "Spring!" yarked Angus, and "Play!" yarked Sadie.

But spring had begun long before that day, Toaff thought, even before the human had chainsawed his pine into pieces. How could the dogs not know that?

The mate pulled down one of the branches and put her

nose into it. Then she stretched her front leg up into the tree to grab a higher branch.

Toaff fled up the trunk.

The mate let the branch go and it snapped back, shorter than it had been. She had broken it, like the wind breaking off the top of the dead pine. She reached out again.

Toaff couldn't go any higher.

"Flowers," yarked Sadie, but Angus knew better. "Blossoms," he told her, then Sadie yarked a question, "Sure?" and Angus answered, "Yes."

The mate pulled down on a branch. *What if I—?*

Toaff ran down the other side of the trunk to go past the reaching paw, but then, *What if she—?* He ran back up.

"Squirrel!" yarked Sadie, and the mate broke a second branch. "Squirrel?" Sadie asked.

The mate turned around and spoke to the dogs and Angus yarked, "Come!"

"Hello, squirrel!" Sadie yarked, and they all went away.

It was not much later that Toaff heard the dogs again, this time in the distance. "Go!" Angus yarked. "Go there." His voice was bossy and his yarking was answered by voices Toaff had never heard before. The sounds came from off beyond the nest-barn, many voices, all mixed together, all saying the same thing, whatever *that* was.

Sadie yarked, "Do what Angus says! And me, too!"

Those new voices made a sound full of *bau*. Angus yarked, "No! Go *there*!" and *bau-bau-bau*, the animals answered, but not as if they were complaining, or frightened, or hungry. It sounded as if the animals just wanted to be making their noise. Gradually, all the voices faded away into the distance, and however hard Toaff listened, he could no longer hear them.

All of that was strange and wonderful enough, but the next day something even stranger and more wonderful happened. The next day, when a bright sun had had all morning to warm the air, the mate returned. She brought Sadie with her and something dangled off of one of her front legs. Although, now that Toaff thought of it, humans always went about on their back legs, so Toaff didn't know if the front things were actually legs at all.

The mate and the dog were followed by a small animal, which Toaff thought must be human as well because it, too, moved on its back legs and, like the mate, had a round furry head and no tail. From his perch among the leaves and flowers-or-blossoms, watching the three of them, he couldn't help noticing how frequently the small human fell over. When that happened, the mate helped it back up.

With all that falling and helping, their progress across the grass was so slow that Toaff had to conclude that they had no predators to watch out for. Any squirrel who moved that slowly wouldn't last long. He watched their approach, wondering what the mate was up to now, trying to decide if he needed to flee. "Pik-ik," Sadie yarked to the small human, and Toaff wondered what she was talking about. The mate sat down right under his tree and pulled out of the thing she carried what must have been food, since in not very long they were putting it into their mouths. So humans carried their stores around with them, Toaff thought. He wondered if that was something a squirrel might want to try to do, although he didn't see how. He kept on watching. You never knew when you might learn something useful.

He saw that a lot of the little one's food fell into the grass. When that happened, the mate gave it some more. He saw that sometimes the little one pushed its food into Sadie's face. "*Sturf,*" said Sadie. "*Sturf, sturf,*" as the food was shoved into her mouth. So humans ate what dogs ate, Toaff thought.

Watching the little one feed the dog, the mate made noises as if she was trying to cough, *gha-gha.* When Sadie's long tongue came out to lick her own nose clean, the little one clapped its front paws together. Then Sadie stuck her nose into the little one's face and licked. The big one said *gha-gha* and Sadie yarked, "Good!" They sat eating like that for a while, after which the little one began to wander around. The little one tried to run after Sadie, and when it fell over, the dog would come back to lick at its face, and then the little one would cough, too, *gha-gha-gha,* and the big one would cough and Sadie would jump back and forth. "Play!"

Angus interrupted them. "Come on, Sadie!" he yarked.

"Not now," Sadie answered. "Helping Missus and baby."

Baby? Was the little one a baby? A human baby? Toaff hadn't known that humans had babies, like squirrels did.

"Mister said!" yarked Angus.

Was Mister the other big human in the white nest-house?

"Not now!" Sadie yarked, then she asked, "Why?"

All the yarking drove the baby back to the Missus mate with the kind of unhappy sounds any frightened baby animal makes. Missus said something loud and the dogs went away and then, in a day filled with surprises, the most surprising thing of all happened. Missus began to talk, but not in the voice she had used before. This new talking was that long line of sound the color of squirrels' tails, or silver moonlight. Missus talked and talked, winding the line of sound around her baby, and the baby grew quiet. It nestled up close to her until she wrapped her front legs around it, like a long, soft tail. Then she stopped the new talking, stood up, reached down for the thing she kept her stores in, and carried her baby across to the nest-house.

Not until then did Toaff notice the smell. Something that smelled like a squirrel could eat it had been left behind in the grass under his tree. He scurried down and found a few apple bits and some crumbs of the soft white food. Toaff ate until he was full enough, then decided to carry the extra up to his den. They could be stores for him. They wouldn't be as long-lasting as nuts and seeds, he knew, but still, they would be food for the next day or two.

He was coming back down for his second mouthful when the crows arrived. *Kaah-kaah!* called the two crows who flew down to land just under Toaff's tree.

What a day this was! Toaff had never been so close to a crow before. They were bigger than he'd thought and their black feathers lay smooth as sky against their bodies. They kept pointing at the ground with their black beaks, until he had to whuffle and call out to them, "I know, I already know. But thank you."

They didn't even look up. They *kaah-kaah*ed quietly, as if discussing something. Then, moving along the hoppy way crows do, their heads jabbing forward with every hop, they came out from under the blossom-or-flower-filled branches, spread their wings, and rose up, into the air, calling back to him, *Kaah-kaah!* Maybe to say, *What are you waiting for?*

But when Toaff stood in the grass under his tree, the food was gone. All of it.

# CROWS AND CATS

Missus didn't reappear for many days after that. During that time the flowers-or-blossoms had fallen off their branches, drifting down onto the grass to lie there, quiet as snow, until gentle breezes gradually blew them away. Bright green leaves uncurled on the apple trees. Day after day, night after night, the air warmed. The days grew longer, too, and the nights shorter.

But when Toaff squeezed out of his den one morning to forage, there Missus was. She stood in the same entrance and once more pieces of white food flew out from her front legs. Before she had finished, the crows were flying at her, *kaah-kaah*ing, and when she had gone back into her nest-house, the crows landed.

That was when Toaff saw it. A solitary gray squirrel was approaching from around the far corner. A gray squirrel! His heart danced at the sight. It *was* a gray squirrel, who might have come from those trees beyond, so he jumped up from his perch to scramble down the trunk and dash across the grass to greet it. Sharp *kaah-kaahs* stopped him, maybe saying *Go away!* Or *Mine!* Toaff couldn't understand crows, so they could just as easily have been greeting the squirrel, asking, *What took you so long?* The crows flew noisily off, and at that moment two cats came creeping along his side of the nest-house, where the other Gray couldn't see them.

Toaff chuk-chukked a warning, screeching, "Cats! Run! Cats!"

Without even looking to see who had sounded the alarm, the other squirrel spun around and fled.

Their prey lost, both cats sat in the grass in front of the nest-house entrance. They licked their paws, slowly and carefully, over and over. They didn't eat the food. They

didn't even smell it. They just sat on food some other animal could have had if they hadn't been there. They just sat and rubbed at their ears and licked their paws, waiting, and Toaff had a sudden, unexpected, unpleasant idea: Did the *kaah-kaahs* tell the cats that squirrels would be out foraging?

The next time Missus stepped into the entrance to scatter food, two crows flew noisily at her and Toaff stayed away. He watched. Maybe the crows were greeting her, or driving her back inside, maybe they were telling any nearby squirrel there was food, or maybe they were announcing to the cats that a squirrel would appear. He needed to know what was going on before he ran out across the grass, beyond shelter. That day, no cats appeared and no squirrels either, and the crows ate everything. The time after that, however, not one crow was around to *kaah-kaah* the news to the cats, if that was what they did. So Toaff scurried down, to forage.

He found fat chunks of the soft, satisfying food waiting in the grass. He had time to gobble one down, sitting up on his haunches, looking all around while he chewed hurriedly, and he had just picked up another when he saw the gray squirrel, rounding the corner of the nest-house, and was there another squirrel, too?

Because he was watching the squirrel, Toaff didn't see the cat. In fact, the first warning he had of it was the sudden cry of a squirrel. "Cat!" it chukked, but not to warn Toaff. It was calling back over its shoulder as it wheeled around. "Cat! Let's go!" and it disappeared from sight.

Toaff had no chance of making it back to his apple tree. The cat was approaching from that same direction. It would easily cut him off. And finish him off.

Just behind him was the entrance that Missus came out of. Toaff dropped the food and jumped, up, up one flat piece of wood and then again, up another. At the top he ran into a solid wall.

How had Missus gone into her nest through a solid wall?

He had no time to wonder about that, and besides, who knew what humans could do? He leaped, landed hard, and ran, ran fast, to get away from the cat. He followed that other squirrel, racing alongside the nest-house and around the corner, and there *were* trees! Trees close by! Toaff raced up the trunk of the first tree he came to. This was a maple, not that that mattered, although for some reason it made him feel a little less panicky to be back in a maple tree. At a high branch he stopped, his heart thumping, to look back.

The cat was already climbing up the trunk, moving fast. Toaff scrambled higher. Squirrels climb more nimbly than cats, so he wasn't too worried about being caught. Without deciding—because he had already decided it as soon as he rounded the corner and saw three tall trees—Toaff ran along a branch and leaped across to the next tree. This was also a maple, and when he looked back a second time, what he saw came as a pleasant surprise.

Cats might be sleek and fast on the ground, and yes, they were good climbers, but they couldn't leap from one tree to the next, and getting down a tree trunk was difficult for a cat. Toaff saw the cat now climbing backward down the maple trunk, one stiff, clumsy, anxious step after another. It was digging its claws into the trunk and its tail dragged on the bark and Toaff whuffled at the sight.

The cat heard him, of course. It was still well above the ground, but it stopped to glare at the squirrel who got away. It glared and hissed softly, then returned to the work of clambering down. Once on the grass, it looked up at Toaff, who was watching from his safe perch. The cat's long tail waved back and forth, slowly. "I'll remember you," it hissed.

Toaff had never been hissed at before. Hissing made the words hard to understand. "What?" he asked. "What did you say?"

"You don't think you can snark at a cat, do you?" hissed the big white animal, but more slowly so that Toaff *did* understand. He didn't feel like whuffling now. He backed up. The leaves on the maple were new and small but they might protect him from the hissing cat.

"I'm Fox," the cat hissed after him, and it wasn't until Toaff was safely on the opposite side of the tree's trunk, huddled up against a sturdy branch, that he thought to wonder: Why would a cat be called Fox? The cat hissed, "I'm Fox, and sooner or later, probably sooner, you're going to make me a good dinner."

Toaff peered around to see that the cat had seated himself next to the nest-house. His blue eyes were fixed on him. The tail stroked back and forth along the grass.

Cats were patient, Toaff knew. Squirrels were not, and he was a squirrel. Already he could feel panic quivering in his paws, a panic that made him want to dash and hope, dash down the trunk and back to the apple trees, hoping with every bound that the cat wouldn't get him. He forced himself to stay still, even though anxious questions—*What will I eat?* and *Where will I sleep?* and *When will he go away?*—raced around and around inside his head, circling faster and faster, crying in sharper and louder voices. Toaff dug his nails into the branch and stayed right where he was.

It was a long time before Toaff moved at all and that was just to hide himself farther along the maple branch, deeper among its small leaves. That was when he saw that the third tree was an oak. Oaks, Toaff had heard often enough, meant acorns in the fall. In the fall any squirrel who found himself living near an oak was in luck for the winter.

But it was spring now and Fox was still waiting. His tail still swept back and forth, back and forth. Toaff began thinking about the stores in his little den back in the apple tree. How long could the cat sit there? Just waiting. Too long, much too long. The jittery feeling moved all the way up his legs and he had to move. He leaped across to the oak, and when he looked down again, Fox had left, and Toaff, lighthearted with relief, leaped back to the first maple. He felt as weightless as wind and as strong as any tree and he made up his mind. There were squirrels somewhere on this side of the nest-house and he was a squirrel who had just escaped from a cat: He would stay here. With two maples and an oak, there was bound to be somewhere for a squirrel to live. For the first time, he looked up. He glimpsed a large and untidy nest, like a small and rather dirty cloud trapped in the high branches of the maple closest to the nest-house.

What kind of a bird would build a nest so badly?

Something round appeared at the untidy edge of the nest above him.

It was the head of a squirrel. It was the round head of a gray squirrel. A second head joined the first, and then a third.

Toaff didn't know what to think.

"That was some good jumping," one said.

"We saw you before," another added. "Your tail is so silver, and didn't you warn me once?"

By then, Toaff *did* know what he ought to think. "Is that a drey?" he asked.

"Do we live in it?" the third asked, then, "Are we squirrels?" and finally, "How stupid are you?"

"Come on up," the first two heads chukked. "There's lots of room."

# INTRODUCING THE LUCKY ONES

When Toaff tumbled into the drey, three squirrels waited there, sitting in a row.

"Hello," he said.

"You got away from Fox," said the smallest one in an admiring voice.

Toaff didn't want to boast. "I was lucky."

"Did you hear that?" she asked the other two.

What was there to hear? Toaff wondered as he told them, "I'm Toaff."

"You made Fox really angry," said the squirrel in the middle. He had a long white scar running from his neck down over his shoulder to his belly.

Toaff couldn't help staring at the scar. He told himself it wasn't smart to ask a squirrel who hadn't even told you his name how he got his scar. In any case, "There's nothing special about making Fox angry, Tzaaf," said the third squirrel, who was the largest. "Fox hates not getting what he wants."

"I *know* that," Tzaaf answered.

The first squirrel ignored the quarreling. "I'm Mroof,"

she said. Her pale gray tail waved gently behind her. She was the softest-looking creature Toaff had ever seen, with fur the color of the clouds that carry friendly little spring rains. She reminded him of Soaff. "And that's Tzaaf and that's Pneef. Don't mind her."

"Hello," Toaff said again. He saw how large the drey was, to give squirrels plenty of room for play, and how high its woven walls rose, to keep squirrels out of bad weather, and how thick were the branches above, to protect squirrels from flying predators. "How many of you live here?" he asked.

"Three," Mroof answered. "Do you want to stay?"

It might have been big but Toaff didn't see any stores, so he decided, "I have my own nest."

As he was saying that, Pneef was protesting, "Mroof! You can't invite just anybody!"

"Where is it?" Tzaaf asked. "It must be somewhere near because I've seen you. You warned me about the cat, didn't you?"

"It's in the apple tree. I was watching from there."

"I suppose you'll tell everybody about our drey, now you've seen it," Pneef decided. "He will," she assured the others, and predicted, "And they'll all come here to live. The humans won't like that."

Why was Pneef so unfriendly? That was another reason not to stay. "There isn't any everybody," Toaff said. "And I like my tree. It had flowers all over it, for days and days. Or maybe they were blossoms," he added.

"They were blossoms," Pneef told him, sounding just like Braff, as if she knew everything and he didn't know anything. "Why isn't there any everybody?" she demanded. "I told you there was something funny about him," she said to Tzaaf and Mroof.

Mroof disagreed. "Squirrels can live alone," she said. "Don't you remember? The rest told us that before they left last fall, before we went into the nest-house for the winter after Tzaaf got better. So there's nothing wrong with there being just one squirrel in a nest."

Especially *my* nest, Toaff thought, unable to imagine what it might be like to try to squeeze even a mouse into that tiny den.

Mroof explained it to him. "Pneef is just being careful. She's always careful."

"I'd still like to hear why he's alone," Pneef insisted. "Unless you have something to hide?" she asked Toaff.

"I don't," Toaff said. "My other den was big, bigger than this drey. I think our nest in that den was as big as this whole drey, and there was another nest, just as big, to fit in all the other squirrels, and there was still room for piles of stores so that when everything was covered with snow, or if there was a storm, or even in early spring, we would all have enough. There were two mothers and two litters, and some adult males. I had two littermates. We were older than the other ones."

"Where are they all now?" Pneef asked.

"I don't know. Maybe behind the nest-barn."

"The nest-barn is all the way around the corner. Past the garden," Pneef told him. "We don't go there. There's nothing useful about the nest-barn."

"Then why do the humans have it?" wondered Toaff, who was tired of being told things.

"They'll have a reason," she answered quickly. "It will be a good reason."

"Like there's a reason for the cats," Mroof said, "which is to keep mice out of the nest-house. Humans don't like mice."

Not to be outdone, Tzaaf added, "And the reason for dogs is to keep out raccoons."

"But the humans don't let the dogs hunt squirrels," Mroof said.

Tzaaf wasn't sure about that. "You can't tell what dogs will do. Especially Angus."

"Dogs don't eat squirrels," Pneef announced.

"They might if they were hungry," Tzaaf argued.

Toaff was glad to hear that someone else didn't always agree with Pneef.

"That's why the humans feed them," Pneef said.

"Then why do they chase us?" Tzaaf asked. "Especially that Sadie."

Toaff had an idea about that, but he kept it to himself. He didn't know if these squirrels liked to hear new ideas.

Mroof ignored this little quarrel to explain, "The dogs

keep us safe from the raccoons, who *would* hunt us, if it wasn't for the dogs."

"What do raccoons look like?" Toaff asked her. She seemed friendlier than the other two.

"You'll know them when you see them," Pneef predicted.

"They don't come near our trees," Mroof promised. "We're the Lucky Ones about raccoons, just like about everything else. And I think Toaff's a Lucky One, too," she told Pneef and Tzaaf. Then she whuffled. "Did you hear that? *One two.*"

Everyone except Toaff whuffled with her, and Tzaaf added, "If he is, he'd be *one four*," which set them off again. Toaff sat there, thinking that maybe he wanted to leave. Maybe he would do that, even if this drey was so large and safe, even if he didn't really want to return to his cramped den in the apple tree. Even if he had just realized that he was tired of being just one squirrel, alone. To be an only alone was different from being an only among others. So he waited a little longer, to see what would happen next if he stayed.

# TOAFF MAKES A CHOICE

Next Mroof asked him, "Why aren't you still living with all of those others?" She sounded as if she was curious to hear, not curious to find out something wrong with him, so Toaff answered.

"Our den was in the hollow center of a dead pine. One night last winter, in that really big storm—do you remember that really big one?"

"We were inside all winter," Tzaaf said, and he said it proudly.

"Inside?" Toaff asked. "With the humans? In the nest-house?"

"At the very top, right under its top."

"We found it ourselves and we stayed," Pneef added.

"Humans want us to be safe in winter weather," Mroof said.

Toaff looked through the branches and leaves at the dark, slanted cover of the nest-house. No storm would break that nest-house in half, or blow snow into it. "You *are* lucky," he said.

"We told you," Pneef told him.

"Our tree was broken by that storm," Toaff said. "When I woke up in the morning, the others had all gone away. I didn't know where they were."

"Why didn't they take you with them, then?" asked Pneef.

This was the first time Toaff had remembered that night. Squirrels have to remember what's important, like where to forage and how to get back to the nest and what's dangerous. They remember stories, too, but for another reason. Unimportant things—every single place they buried food last fall, for example, or who said what mean thing to them, or even things they wish hadn't happened—those, they mostly forget right away. Toaff said, "I expect they didn't see me. Or maybe they thought I was dead? I remember everything being dark and loud all around me and then I wasn't awake anymore and in the morning they were all gone. The den had turned upside down and the stores were scattered everywhere. So I made a new nest and piled up the stores again. Why would I leave?"

"If that's true," Pneef insisted, "why did you tell us they might be living behind the nest-barn?"

"One of my littermates came back for stores and he told me. He said I could go with him, but I didn't want to."

"If there was so much food there, why did you leave *that* den?" asked Pneef.

If it had been Braff who kept asking these questions, as if Toaff was saying something that wasn't true, Toaff would have stuck his nose right under his littermate's front leg and snuffled until it turned into a wrestling-snuffling-whuffling match. But this was Pneef and he didn't know how to convince her he wasn't making anything up. He wanted to convince her because remembering the big den in the dead pine made him want to sleep again in a pile of warm squirrel bodies, at least for one night. So he explained.

"When all the snow had melted, the human came and cut my broken tree up into pieces. With a chain saw. The dogs were there, too."

"That was a lawn mower," Tzaaf told him. "He uses a lawn mower to cut things."

Then Pneef asked, "Why didn't you go to find the others, if you knew where they were?"

"The apple tree was closer," Toaff said, and that was true. Also true was that he didn't want to live in the same nest with Braff. Then he remembered a better argument. "My littermate came back to tell me they were moving across the road." The Lucky Ones didn't seem to understand what that meant, so he told them, "The road is at the end of the drive and it's more dangerous than anyplace else on the farm. Everybody said. Machines on the road are a lot more dangerous than they are on the drive."

After a short silence, "I think Toaff can stay," Mroof announced. "What if the reason the humans cut up his pine tree was so he would have to leave it, and find us?"

"Maybe. But what if they were trying to get rid of his whole den but he escaped?" Pneef argued.

"*And* he had all those stores to eat at the end of winter. *And* he found a nest in the apple tree."

"I found a den," Toaff corrected. He wanted Mroof to know the exact true way things had been. "I built my own nest. It's small, because the den is so small," he admitted.

Tzaaf had made up his mind. "I agree with Mroof. I think he's supposed to be a Lucky One."

"I can help forage," Toaff offered, which set them off whuffling again.

"Why would we need help foraging when the humans feed us?" Pneef asked. "Look," she said, and led him to the high edge of the drey. Mroof and Tzaaf followed. The four squirrels stood in a row on their back legs to peer through leaves in the direction of the white nest-house.

"See that little nest-house on a pole? With a roof of its own?"

What Toaff saw looked like a thin young tree with not one single branch on it. At its top was a nest no bigger than his den in the apple tree, without walls but with its own top, like a human nest. Its floor was covered by yellowy-brown bumps.

"That's our feeder," Tzaaf announced.

"Those are seeds in it," Mroof told him. "Have you ever tasted seeds? If you haven't? You'll see, they taste better than anything."

"The humans keep the feeder full of seeds for us," Pneef told him.

"We share it with the birds," Tzaaf said, and while they stood watching, a robin flew down from high in their maple to land in the feeder. For a few minutes, it perched there, pecking and eating.

Mroof explained, "Humans want us to share."

"Do the crows eat there too?" Toaff wondered. He never would have guessed that crows were good sharers.

"Not crows," Pneef told him. "Why would humans care about crows? It's the nice birds they want us to share with, the sparrows and robins, the juncos, the warblers. Nobody cares about crows."

Toaff did, but he decided not to say what he was thinking, because squirrels don't like to be told things they don't agree with. When you lived alone, he thought, nobody quarreled. He wondered if he wouldn't prefer to go back to his own den after all. But the Lucky Ones had more to tell him.

"The humans like to watch us eat," Mroof said. "Sometimes when we are eating? They come to an entrance and knock on it, to say hello."

"When it's winter they hang suet on the low branches, because suet keeps you warm in the cold," Tzaaf told him.

Toaff couldn't imagine any of this. This was too wonderful to be believed: a big drey to live in, food put out for you, being warm inside a human nest all winter long, and other squirrels to play with and tell stories with. Maybe he would have to be careful not to argue, but even so, he *did* want to live here. Also, he could tell that Mroof really wanted him to stay and he liked being wanted.

"We're the Lucky Ones," Mroof said, again, "and you're probably one too, because you got away from Fox. So you should stay." They returned to sitting in the drey, but this time the three of them were all spread around, not in a row, and even Pneef agreed, sort of.

"We can try him," she said.

# HOW TZAAF GOT HIS SCAR

Spring days were warm. In spring, even the rain fell warm. The Lucky Ones, and Toaff, spent the sunny hours playing chase-me and find-me, or jumping from tree to tree, racing around trunks, then jumping again, with frequent stops at the feeder. The humans and the dogs were sometimes outside and sometimes inside, but they didn't bother the squirrels. The one danger was the cats, but the squirrels all kept a watchful eye out and, really, nothing interfered with their enjoyment of each spring day.

Toaff had never had such a comfortable life. He hoped that he was showing them he really belonged in their drey. The longer he was there, the more he wanted to stay. He noticed as much as he could about how they thought Lucky Ones should act so he could be that, too, so they would feel he was just like them.

He himself felt most like a real Lucky One on those occasional rainy days, or when a chilly wind blew, and they all stayed in the dry warmth of the drey to chuk about one thing or another, or tell stories. The Lucky Ones knew a lot of stories, some of them familiar to Toaff and some new.

He listened happily to all of them, without saying anything. On the third such day, Toaff finally asked about Tzaaf's scar. It was Tzaaf's story, but it was Mroof who told it.

"I was in the drey and Pneef was here with me, but everyone else wasn't because they wanted to see if behind the nest-barn was a safer place than here, because of the cats. We weren't yet strong enough to go so far. Tzaaf thought he saw Missus putting out bread, and he wanted to have some before the crows took it, and we told him not to go, but he didn't listen. We did, we warned you," Mroof said to Tzaaf, who seemed to be about to protest.

Tzaaf kept quiet.

Mroof said, "So we saw Snake first, because he came along our side of the nest-house, when Tzaaf was just going around the corner. We chukked, as loud as we could, both of us, together. We made a lot of noise," she told Toaff proudly. "And he heard us."

"But Snake was between me and the trees," Tzaaf told Toaff.

"Scary," Toaff said. "Really scary. How'd you get away?"

Tzaaf shook his head and shifted his position, to show Toaff his whole long scar.

"He didn't," Mroof said. "He couldn't. A young squirrel has no chance to outrun a cat and there were no trees to climb. We wanted to help, but what could we do? It was terrible because we knew what would happen. It was worse than terrible because it didn't happen right away. At first, Tzaaf was too frightened to move. We could see that and we didn't blame him one bit. Snake was crouched down in front of Tzaaf, and his tail was waving and he hissed. He liked watching Tzaaf be so frightened, so he didn't spring right away."

"He just hissed at me," Tzaaf added.

Toaff could imagine how the squirrel must have felt, just waiting for the cat to spring, that hissing voice and those staring eyes. "What happened? How did you—?"

"Then Snake attacked!" Mroof said. "We could see his claws, even from up here, and Tzaaf screamed!"

Pneef spoke then, to say, "That was the worst thing, when he was screaming."

Toaff had heard that mouse's cry and mice were littler than squirrels, a lot littler and much quieter too. He could imagine what Mroof and Pneef had seen, and heard.

"But Missus *had* been there! Tzaaf was right, she *was* putting out food. She said something loud. She was much louder than us, wasn't she, Pneef? But Snake didn't pay any attention to her, but then Mister came through the entrance and the dogs came yarking, both of them, yarking and yarking, and Mister was carrying something and he threw brown water from it down on Snake and Tzaaf, and Snake hated that. He backed up, hissing. Hissing at Mister! We thought he was going to attack Mister, he was that mad."

"He had his back all arched and his hair was sticking out," Pneef added.

"But Mister just said something loud and waved what he was carrying at Snake—"

"But no more brown water came out—"

"—and Snake ran away. Humans can make cats do what they want them to, because they're so big," Mroof explained. "So Tzaaf was saved." She waited a minute before she said, "But Tzaaf didn't stand up."

"I couldn't," Tzaaf said. "I can't even remember what happened, I was just . . . afraid and . . . I couldn't move. They were right there, both of the humans, and looking at me and their voices were so loud. . . ."

That, Toaff didn't *want* to imagine.

"But you know what Missus did?" Mroof asked. "Missus sat right down beside Tzaaf, but not too close, and she stayed sitting there."

"Looking at me," Tzaaf added.

"We came as far down the trunk as we dared," Mroof said. "We were calling to you, remember?"

"Telling you to get up, asking you if you were dead," Pneef said.

"Which I wasn't, but it began to hurt, and I could smell my own blood. And after a while, I *could* get up and I could go over to the tree and climb it, and I don't know how I did that, but I did it." There was amazement in his voice as he said, "I think Missus wanted to watch me until I was safe. I think that's why she sat there."

"So Snake wouldn't come back. Or Fox," Mroof said.

Toaff said, "You're lucky to be alive, Tzaaf."

Tzaaf nodded his agreement. "I only am because Missus and Mister helped me, because they take care of us."

"So when the rest didn't come back and we couldn't go after them because Tzaaf couldn't climb down, or run, or jump," Mroof said, "we stayed too. They said they'd come back before winter."

"They said they'd come back but they never did," Pneef told him. "So we know something bad must have happened to them. It was lucky we didn't go with them."

"Which is another reason we're the Lucky Ones," Mroof concluded.

"You certainly are," Toaff agreed. He wanted to be there too, with them in that drey, being lucky.

# TWO MORE STORIES,
# AT LEAST ONE OF THEM TRUE

In the drey, in the company of the Lucky Ones, Toaff didn't mind a rainy day. The Lucky Ones knew all kinds of stories and Toaff of course never said he already knew some of them. Squirrels never mind hearing a good story over and over, especially the oldest ones, about squirrels so long dead that nobody could even say what part of the farm they had inhabited. Their favorite old story was the one about swimming squirrels.

In the story, the squirrels crossed a pond to escape a family of foxes that had moved into their woods. "They could swim—well, all squirrels can," said Mroof. "Just, most of us don't want to have to. But those squirrels ran right into the water and swam, and it was nighttime, too, but the moon made a path, to show them the way. They swam and swam and they were getting tired, especially the babies. Then the old wise squirrel, the same one who knew about the woods across the pond, had another idea."

"It wasn't him," Pneef corrected her. "It was the youngest one. It's always the youngest ones who have the new ideas."

"You're both wrong. It was a mother, because the babies were in danger," said Tzaaf.

Toaff knew what a pond was—a gigantic puddle. He was picturing what it would look like—squirrels crossing a pond at night in the silver moonlight. He didn't care who had had the idea. Old Criff hadn't ever told that part and Toaff thought the story was better without it.

"That wise old squirrel raised his tail up, out of the water," Mroof said. "He raised it up high and spread it out wide and the wind blew at it from behind and pushed him forward."

"It was the youngest one who did that," Pneef repeated.

"No, it was one of the mothers," Tzaaf insisted.

"*Then*," Mroof said loudly, with a stern look first at Pneef and then at Tzaaf, "they *all* raised their tails and spread them out wide and the wind pushed all of them forward, to their new territory, on the opposite bank."

That could happen. Toaff could imagine how it might work. But he wondered, "Didn't the foxes chase after them?" In his experience, foxes didn't give up easily.

"Foxes can't swim," Mroof declared. Then she asked, "Can they?"

"They don't have fat tails either," Tzaaf said. "Do they?"

The Lucky Ones had never seen a fox, so Toaff could tell them, "They have long, bushy tails but I don't know about the swimming."

"You've seen a fox? Weren't you afraid?"

"Humans aren't afraid of foxes, did you know that?"

"Humans aren't afraid of anything."

"You saw a real fox?"

So Toaff had his own story to tell, first about a fox tracking a mouse under the snow and then about how to save a mouse from a fox. After that he started to tell them about escaping from the orange-headed giant with his chain saw. "That must have been Mister," they explained.

"Did he have Angus with him? The black-and-white dog?"

"Nobody but Mister would know how to cut a tree into pieces."

"So I fled. To look for a nest in the apple trees," Toaff concluded.

"I've been there," Pneef said. "They're not fit to live in. You're lucky we found you."

"But it wasn't a chain saw," Tzaaf told him. "It was a lawn mower. A lawn mower is what Mister uses to cut the grass. That's his cutting-down tool. It makes a lot of noise, just the way you described, but on this side of the nest-house it doesn't stop until it's finished."

"He'd never use it on *our* trees," Mroof promised them all. "Or on the feeder either," she added because she wanted it to be true. "Otherwise, how would they be sure we had food when there's snow?"

Maybe it *was* a lawn mower, not a chain saw, Toaff thought. Why would Braff know the name of a machine better than these Lucky Ones? Except, he thought, why would these squirrels, who never went far from their own drey, know more than Braff?

But he knew better than to ask the Lucky Ones those questions.

# THE LUCKY ONES
# EXPLAIN EVERYTHING

The question was soon settled in Braff's favor when the four squirrels watched Mister follow a noisy machine around and around on the grass near his nest-house. He held on to its two long legs so it wouldn't get away from him as it whined and pulled and sometimes cried out with a quick sharp sound. Most of the time it just whined, on and on, for so long that Toaff wanted to run off, run away, run anywhere, just to escape the sound of it. This was not a chain saw and Toaff was glad to be able to tell something to the Lucky Ones. "If that's the lawn mower, the chain saw is something else," he told them, when the machine had finally pulled Mister around the corner to continue its whining somewhere farther off.

"Can you believe how stubborn he is?" Pneef asked Mroof and Tzaaf. Then she asked Toaff, in the kind of voice a mother uses with her baby when he is being very silly, "Why would a human need two different machines for cutting things down?"

"I don't know that, but the machine that cut down my tree didn't look or sound like this one, and they told me it was a chain saw," Toaff answered.

"What they?" Pneef asked. "They who? Do those theys of yours live close to humans like we do?" She turned to Tzaaf and Mroof and said, "He always thinks he knows better than us."

Toaff didn't understand why Pneef thought that. Had he argued when the Lucky Ones told him rules? ("Don't chase birds away from the feeder, the humans want to see them." "Don't come too close to the nest-house, they don't like that." "Do what we tell you, we know what humans want.") No, he hadn't argued, not one word, even though he sometimes wanted to. Some of the rules made no sense. Why *shouldn't* a squirrel forage at night if he was hungry? Why *were* they supposed to stay away from the humans, who must want them to stay close, because otherwise why would they put out so much food? Why have a rule about the dogs' food if you never saw the dogs eating?

The reason he didn't argue was simple: The Lucky Ones didn't like to be disagreed with and Toaff wanted to be one of the Lucky Ones. He wanted to live in the drey high up in the maple tree. He wanted to eat at the feeder. That was why he didn't insist about the chain saw even though he now knew for sure there were two different machines. But why couldn't Toaff be right about even one thing? Why couldn't he have his own idea about some one thing?

Every time he turned around, it seemed, there was another rule. "Don't leave this side of the nest-house."

"I used to live on the other side," Toaff pointed out.

"And look what happened," Pneef said.

Tzaaf explained, "If they wanted us on the other side, they wouldn't have Snake and Fox living over there."

Mroof added, "This is the nicest side. And the safest. And it has the feeder."

"You can go anywhere you want to, on this side," Tzaaf told him.

"Except an entrance," Pneef said, so quickly that Toaff began to be curious about what there might be, after an entrance, inside. He wondered but did not ask, even though if any squirrels knew the answer to that question, it would be the Lucky Ones.

"We don't want to bother the humans. Not ever," Pneef told him, with so stern a look that he wondered if she could somehow hear everything he didn't say out loud. "For one thing, humans take care of us and we're grateful. But also, imagine what they could do if they got angry."

"What would they do?" Toaff wondered.

"I don't want to find out," Tzaaf said.

"Whatever they do, it's because they want to take care of us," Mroof explained, adding, "Anyway, I'm hungry. Is anyone else hungry?"

Toaff followed them out of the drey without saying anything more. He didn't want to quarrel with the Lucky Ones. Maybe they didn't know as much as they thought they did, but they were right about one thing—they were definitely lucky.

# SUMMER

# TOAFF BREAKS THE RULE

When *day* became a word that stretched out so far ahead of them that there was time for everything, eating and playing and chattering and leaping, the squirrels knew that summer had arrived. "Well," they said to one another and "I guess," before they went back to eating and playing and chattering and leaping. Toaff enjoyed all of those things, and he enjoyed the company of others, but he also kept wondering about those entrances. Of course he was curious. He didn't know what they were *for*, because the humans went in and out of just one of them, but why else would they want to make so many holes in the walls of their nest? Of course he remembered that he had been told to stay away, and he stayed away. Just as of course, he kept on wondering.

He even saw how a squirrel could get right up to an entrance. One branch of the oak tree reached almost all the way to the white wall of the nest-house. It stretched out so close to one of the high entrances that at night the yellow light from inside spilled out to glisten like rain on its leaves. Toaff knew that if he went to the end of that branch, he'd be able to look inside and see . . . see what? See what the humans did inside their huge nest-house? See why they needed such a large place to live, when they weren't all that big? Maybe even see why they needed so many entrances? How could Toaff help but wonder?

"I don't think we can trust him," Pneef said. "Look at his eyes."

"Toaff has happy eyes," Mroof argued. "He does, and everyone knows that's lucky."

"Lucky for who?" asked Pneef.

Toaff couldn't see his own eyes so he didn't know about happy, but he knew Pneef was smart not to trust him.

But all those entrances didn't make sense, and when something doesn't make sense, a curious squirrel is going to wonder about what he's being told. That was exactly what happened with Toaff. After all, hadn't the Lucky Ones been wrong about the chain saw? Maybe these Lucky Ones didn't know everything about humans either, and maybe the humans wouldn't mind at all if Toaff went up to one of their entrances, just to see what he could see. What harm could there be in him doing that, as long as none of the Lucky Ones knew about it? No harm at all. He was sure of it.

So one hot, drizzly summer afternoon, when the Lucky Ones were all sleeping in the drey, Toaff leaped over to the oak tree and ran along the branch that came so close to the nest-house. He was anxious and excited, and frightened, too, but he reminded himself that he could turn around and disappear among the leaves, quick as anything.

He went out almost to the end of the branch, which

was near enough to jump down to where the bottom of the entrance stuck out, if he dared; but he wasn't sure he wanted to get so close to humans, or break such an important rule. He hesitated among the oak leaves, staring, trying to see into the nest-house. He hesitated, just staring, until he heard it again.

He hadn't heard it for a long time, but Toaff didn't forget the long, silvery sound Missus had made under the apple tree, talking to her baby. She was making it now, inside of her nest-house, just beyond this entrance. Toaff needed to get as close as he could to that sound, which was curling around him and making him feel as safe and glad as he had when he was himself a baby, in the wide nest in the dead pine, ready to fall asleep. The sound wrapped itself around him, and pulled him in.

It was an easy jump onto the entrance's bottom. Toaff landed, balancing on all four paws as he tried to move closer to the sound. But he couldn't move forward. Something was blocking his way. He pushed his nose against it but it didn't move. He could see that it was a thin wall full of tiny openings, too small even for a bug to get through and therefore much too small for a squirrel. All Toaff could do was stand still, right where he was, and listen. So that is what he did.

The silver sound wound around and around him. In the shadowy inside of the nest-house, nothing moved. Peering in, Toaff saw the shape of a human. Missus, he thought, and listened.

Then a dog yarked—a loud, sharp sound—and Sadie burst from the shadows. "Who *yarkyark*? What *yarkyark* doing?" she demanded in fierce growling yarks.

Toaff had never before heard Sadie sound dangerous.

With a chittering of nails on wood, Angus joined her in her yarking. "Get! Away! Out!"

The silver sound stopped. The human inside turned toward Toaff and she saw him. As soon as Missus saw him, she stood stiff, just where she was.

All Toaff could do was stare at her.

She stared right back at him.

For a long, long time that was actually a short time, they stared at one another. Missus had no fur at all on her face. She was a huge thing, Toaff realized, looking up at her. He was looking right into her eyes, unable to think of anything to say although he did want to say something, even just hello, even if she would never understand him.

"Get it, Sadie! Get it!" Angus yarked, and he jumped up at the entrance. His teeth were long and pointy and his head was big enough to push the thin wall out.

Toaff backed off so fast he almost fell. He caught himself just in time to find his balance and turn to leap back into the oak. He ran along the branch, back to the safety of the trunk. There he huddled, quivering with fear and amazement, trying to remember everything.

He wished he had said hello.

For a long time, Toaff sat quietly, thinking. He looked at the nest-house with its many entrances. Faint sounds of human voices came from inside the nest-house, but that long, silvery sound did not happen again. He began to wonder what, seeing him, Missus had seen to stare at like that, without moving, for such a long time.

To look a human straight in the eye? Toaff had never heard of any squirrel doing that, not ever. He didn't know that he had seen anything particular in her eyes but he did know that she had been looking right back at him. Maybe humans really did take care of squirrels, and wanted them to be warm and dry and well fed. Missus had looked right at him, as if she was waiting. Waiting for what? What was a squirrel supposed to do, eye to eye with a human?

# IN TROUBLE, AGAIN

When Toaff at last returned to the drey, "Did you hear the dogs?" Tzaaf asked.

Toaff didn't know what to answer, but he didn't have to because Tzaaf went right on, to tell him, "They must have been around the other side of the nest-house. Probably chasing off the cats."

Toaff didn't dare tell them the dogs were inside the nest-house, chasing *him* off.

It turned out that he didn't have to tell them anything because late that same afternoon, the figure with the big orange head came around the corner of the nest-house and stood looking at the three trees.

"It's Mister," Pneef announced, peering down over the edge of the drey. "What's he carrying?" she asked. "What is he going to do?" She looked suspiciously at Toaff. "Do you know?"

"It's the chain saw," Toaff said, "but I don't know what he'll do with it." Although he had a terrible, sinking feeling that he could guess.

"*That's* a chain saw? What's wrong with Mister's head?"

"Didn't you tell us he cut things up with the chain saw?" Mroof asked. "What is he going to cut up?"

It turned out that Mister was cutting up a branch from the oak tree, and it turned out that it was the long branch that almost touched the side of the nest-house. Mister chainsawed the branch off and then he chainsawed it into pieces and took the pieces away. The Lucky Ones watched this happen, and listened to it happen, and didn't say a single word to one another. They huddled together in the drey, peeping over the edge sometimes, when the screeching stopped. Even though he knew he didn't have the right to do it, Toaff crept in close between Mroof and Tzaaf.

Then Mister returned to reach the chain saw up and cut off another branch, this one from their own maple tree, a branch that also stretched out toward the nest-house, even though it wasn't nearly long enough to reach any entrance. When that branch lay among its leaves on the ground, the chain saw sliced off its smaller branches, then cut it up into chunks, and Mister took all of that away, too.

After that, while the squirrels were still in a shocked silence, he came back again, took off his orange head, and stared right up at their drey.

In a soft, frightened chuk of a voice, Mroof asked, "Is he going to cut our tree down?"

"Why would he do that?" Tzaaf asked.

"That's it exactly," Pneef said. "That's the exact right question: Why?" She gave Toaff one of her looks, then

132

asked point-blank, "Toaff? Can *you* tell us? Why would he do that, Toaff?"

Toaff looked away. He was afraid he was going to have to tell them what had happened. He didn't know how to begin explaining. He knew he would be in trouble.

As it turned out, Toaff didn't have a chance to say anything.

"It *was* Toaff," Pneef announced.

Mister walked away, carrying the chain saw.

"It *has* to be something Toaff did," Pneef said. "While we were asleep and couldn't stop him."

"How could Toaff do anything to make the humans so angry they cut off perfectly good branches?" Tzaaf asked.

Mroof remembered, and now she said, "Toaff was right about the chain saw," as if that was a good argument on Toaff's side of things.

There was no argument on his side that would be good enough.

"I never wanted him to stay," Pneef reminded them.

"Toaff?" Mroof asked.

She was asking him to tell them he had nothing to do with it, but Toaff couldn't say that. He knew he had everything to do with it.

"*Do* you know why?" Tzaaf asked.

Toaff couldn't think of what words to say. He didn't know any words that were sad enough to say how sorry he was.

"Look at his tail," Pneef advised the other two. "He knows something."

Maybe, Toaff thought, if he explained about the silvery sound, maybe they'd understand? And maybe, if they understood, they wouldn't be angry?

Except he knew they must have heard it themselves, at some time, living as close to the nest-house as they did, so he had to know also that they wouldn't understand. They didn't hear what he heard in that silvery sound, and they didn't wonder about the inside of the nest-house, and they didn't want him to know things if *they* didn't already know them. Like the chain saw.

The truth was that he felt as only here as he had in his old den. The truth was that the Lucky Ones were the absolute opposite of only.

Every squirrel except for Toaff was the opposite, he thought sadly; but then he remembered Nilf, who might not be, and that made him remember how Soaff had said she wanted to try leaping, that long-ago winter night.

Then, "Oh, Toaff," Mroof said, in a sad, sad voice.

"He knows it's his fault," Pneef announced.

"But what could Toaff have done to make the humans so angry they cut perfectly good branches off their own trees?" Tzaaf insisted.

Pneef wasn't interested in that, or curious about it. She had decided. "Go away," she said.

When Toaff stayed where he was, too unhappy to move, Pneef's tail flicked. "I *said*, go away," she growled. "Get. Out."

"But, Pneef—" Mroof protested.

"I don't know what he did but I know he did something. Something terrible. This is all *his* fault. Toaff's not a Lucky One and I said so all along. He's un-lucky. I'm right, aren't I, Tzaaf?"

"The humans were never angry before," Tzaaf said. "They never cut off parts of their own trees before. Will they be angry at *us* now? Will they take the feeder away?"

"It was his eyes that fooled you," Pneef explained to Mroof. "I can see how you made the mistake, but he's not lucky, he's just happy, and"—she turned to Toaff—"we don't want you here. None of us do." She turned back to tell the other two, "He has to leave before he ruins everything."

Nobody argued with her. Not even Toaff. He never had belonged here and he'd always known it. He had just hoped he did, and wanted to.

# 26

# FINDING A NEW HOME

There was no point in waiting.

Toaff left without a word of farewell. You don't say, *Thank you, that was fun, see you soon,* to a dreyful of squirrels who have announced they don't want you around. He scrambled over the edge and went down to a branch from which he could jump over to the oak tree. He went around to the other side of the oak's thick trunk, to where the Lucky Ones couldn't see him and he couldn't hear them. Then he sat up on his haunches to try and know what to do.

If he went back to the apple trees, he would have a place to sleep and forage, but he would also have to see and hear the Lucky Ones, and maybe even have to fight to get his share of the food the humans put out. But if he went the other way, he didn't know what to expect. All he knew about the other way was it was the direction the cats came from.

On the other hand, he did know that if it was too dangerous in that unknown part of the farm, he could get back to a safe place.

There was no crow in the sky, maybe telling him what he should do.

Wondering where to go when it was late afternoon already, and wondering how he might travel safely when everything was going to be unfamiliar, Toaff noticed bushes crowding against the bottom of the nest-house. A squirrel could hide among the roots and low branches of bushes. He could run along the ground behind them until he had reached the place where he could see how to get to the stone wall that ran along this side of the farm. In a stone wall there would be openings. A hole just had to be big enough for Toaff's soft and flexible bones to squeeze in. He didn't mind if his nose was out in the open air. No squirrel ever died of a wet nose.

*Do I dare—?*

Toaff ran down the trunk, across the grass, and into the bushes. He didn't stop to look, he didn't look to see, he just ran.

Once under the bushes, he felt safe. For the moment. No predator would want to chase him among this tangle of woody stems with thorns all over them, and stiff leaves. There was a stony smell from the wall of the nest-house, so Toaff went up close to it, to see in the dim light if it offered shelter. It didn't. While it looked like a stone wall, all the spaces between the stones had been filled in with something white, too hard even for a squirrel to gnaw into. This wall offered no shelter. Even so, when he was under the bushes and up against the nest-house, Toaff felt almost as protected as he did perched in a tree's leafy branches, with a solid trunk at his back.

No more than almost, however. Because actually, really, Toaff was not up high and safe. He was down low and possibly in danger. He didn't even know what dangers to look out for, he didn't even know what direction danger might come from. Everything was entirely unfamiliar and he knew he couldn't sleep there, even for one night.

Moving silently, lightly, cautiously, Toaff crossed over and under thorny branches. Every now and then he stopped, sat back on his haunches, and listened. He passed one low narrow entrance and, not long after, another. The entrances were dark but he was taking no chances. If he was seen from inside the nest-house, who knew what might happen? Nothing good, he had learned that much.

When he came to the end of the wall and the end of the bushes, an open space waited in front of him and he could see a stone wall across the drive. That wall disappeared behind a mound of dirt that was so unlikely, and strange, he knew it had to have been made by humans. But why would humans want to pile dirt up? Was this their stores?

Never mind the dirt, he told himself. Never mind the humans. Two scrawny firs grew on the far side of that wall. If he made a dash across the drive, he thought he had a chance of reaching them, he hoped. But he hesitated, listening for a machine, watching for a cat, trying to see any danger that might lie ahead.

Next to the dirt mound he saw a row of short poles,

not far from one another but without feeders on top, and then, turning his head, he saw the nest-barn. The nest-barn? What was the nest-barn doing there?

That was when Toaff understood: The white nest-house was in the middle of everything. Understanding that made up his mind for him and he scurried around the corner, hidden behind two tall, round, smooth-sided things, ready to run across the drive. But this part of the nest-house was a wooden wall that had holes in it, lots and lots of holes.

Why would anyone make a wall with so many small holes in it? Toaff wondered. Could this be the entrance to a squirrel's den? A dark space waited behind the wall-with-holes and, confident that no cat was small enough to squeeze in after him, Toaff stretched himself out thin and entered.

Inside, it was too dark to see but the smell would have blinded him even if he could have. Toaff had never smelled anything so horrible. His eyes burned and watered. The smell choked his nose and his throat. He spun around, to get out, to get out of that dark place with its unbreathable air. For a few panicky heartbeats he couldn't find his way but then he saw the lighted holes and raced to get out before he had to inhale again. That was no squirrel's den. It *stank* of mouse.

Outside, Toaff retreated behind the smooth round things and then back in among the bushes. He sneezed and scratched at his throat with his front paws. He even took a little chew of the bitter bark of a thorny branch. He coughed, and took another little chew. It was dis-*gust*-ing, under the nest-house.

Then he started to whuffle, quietly, all by himself. He liked mice, and he felt sorry for them, being so small and hairless, being such easy prey to any predator. He admired their ability to dart and run and try to survive. And hadn't he once saved a mouse's life? Mice were a good memory to him.

But they sure smelled. Or rather, *and* they sure smelled.

On the other hand, he didn't have to share a nest with them, did he? Or a den, and besides, maybe a squirrel stank just as much to a mouse as a mouse did to a squirrel. He guessed that mice and squirrels should meet up in the open air. Then everything between them would be fine. They could admire one another and help one another out and never have to smell one another.

Cheered by the whuffling, Toaff took a careful look around. *I'm going to—*

He ran, leaping, across the drive—safely!—and through high grass to the stone wall. He crossed the stone wall to the nearer of the fir trees. Searching up and down its trunk, he found a place high up, where a branch had been broken off long enough ago for the space to have been eaten away, first by insects hunting whatever insects ate, and after them by woodpeckers hunting insects. He set to work to enlarge the soft hollow with his sharp teeth.

# A NEW DEN IN A NEW PLACE

It was almost dark before Toaff had scraped a space large enough to be a den. During that time, although he was aware of many sounds, he didn't care what any of them might be. He had to have a den so he never stopped working, not even to forage. That left him to a long, hungry night.

Hunger is no friend to sleep. It stuck itself onto Toaff's tongue and hollowed out his throat. It jabbed its nails into his stomach. Having hard wood under him instead of a soft nest also kept sleep at a distance. And this side of the nest-house was noisy with machine sounds in the drive near the nest-barn and occasional rushing rainwatery sounds from inside the nest-house and always there were human voices, saying who knew what, and the yarking of dogs, and everywhere—or so it seemed to Toaff—the silence of cats.

Toaff dozed and woke until at last he slid into a deep sleep, for how long he couldn't have said, except that it was in a full night darkness that a loud thump smacked down on the black air and made it quiver like a branch seized by the wind.

Toaff jerked awake.

As suddenly as it had come, the thump was gone. A thicker quiet than any Toaff had ever heard before filled the farm, as if every living thing, like the gray squirrel in his tiny den, waited for whatever terrible thing was about to happen. He would have burrowed deeper into the tree if he could have, but he couldn't. He had to stay right where he was, nose out in the air, ears cocked forward, expecting—

Toaff had no idea what that noise might mean.

After a while, low voices spoke, close to the nest-house. These were voices he could understand. Was it squirrels? But these words came in rounded pebbles of sound: These voices *chip-chip*ped, which merely sounded *almost* like squirrels. What did that matter? Because he could understand what they were saying.

"Think they heard?"

"Don't be such a dumbhead, acourse they heard, here come the—"

"Run!"

Growling and snarling and yarking so wildly that Toaff had trouble understanding what they said, the two dogs charged up from the nest-barn. "Where *yark* rrggrrrns?"

"By rrgggrrbg cans, Sadie!"

"I smell rrggrrrns!"

"Thieves! Bad thieves! I see you!"

"Where? Where, Angus?"

"Run, rrggrrrns! Get out!"

A light came on and Mister appeared, without his orange head this time, and said something that made the dogs stop yarking. They ran over to him and he said something else.

"We did a good job!" Sadie yarked.

"Those raccoons won't come back," Angus growled.

Raccoons, Toaff thought. No wonder he could understand what they were saying. But what were raccoons doing that the dogs and human didn't want them to do, so close to the nest-house and in the dark of night?

Curious, he sat in the entrance to his new den, watching, and soon noticed that one of the big round things had fallen over: Was that the *thunk*?

Mister bent over, stood up, and the round things were standing up again, too.

"Garbage *yark* safe," Angus told Sadie.

"We saved the garbage!" she answered happily. "Play?" she yarked.

Mister stood looking down on the garbage—which must have held food of some kind, Toaff decided, since the raccoons were probably out foraging. For a long time the human stood still, not saying anything. Toaff watched the tall black shape, and eventually Mister said something to the dogs.

"Sleep!" Sadie yarked.

"*Whssshshsh*," said Mister.

"Quiet! *Yark* wake baby!" Angus ordered.

"Sleep!" she yarked happily, as if she hadn't understood him.

Toaff whuffled quietly. He was sorry Sadie was a dog, and dangerous to a squirrel. For a while, he wondered why it was that way; then he fell asleep again and was not disturbed until morning.

# A NEW KIND OF DAY

The morning was so busy on this new side of the nest-house that Toaff was trapped in his den until he could figure out how to come out and forage safely. There was a *muuh-muuh*ing call from the nest-barn and Mister went to answer it. When he went in, the dogs ran out, heading for the nest-house, yarking, then they stuck their noses down into something not grass, something the color of a stormy sky.

"Eating!" Sadie yarked. "Eating food! Eating good food!"

"Eat every morning," Angus reminded her.

"Eat good food every morning!" Sadie yarked.

"Just eat," Angus said. "No talking."

Mister emerged from the nest-barn, following two large animals that stepped down heavily and groaned to one another, *muuh-muuh*. Were these the cows Nilf had mentioned? Mister returned to the nest-barn without them, and not much later the machine Toaff had escaped from on that long-ago winter afternoon went down the driveway, carrying Mister away. After another little while, Missus came out of the nest-house, with the baby. The baby fell down in the grass and said *wnaah-wnaah* and Missus made her *gha-gha-gha* coughing sound.

Toaff wondered about this. Like every other baby squirrel, he had not been allowed out of the nest until he could get around easily on his own legs, but Missus just let her baby get up onto its back legs, fall down again, and get up again, without paying much attention. She carried it across the drive, to set it down on more grass while she went off behind the row of poles.

Nothing more moved, so Toaff descended to forage in the empty field by his fir. In the rough grasses that grew around the edge of the field, he found seeds to eat and dew to drink. After eating, he went back up to enlarge his den, so that when he carried up some soft grass, there would be enough room for a nest.

All morning long, noises continued, from machines and humans and dogs, coming and going, nearby and off in the distance. There was also the silent stalking presence of cats. There was the occasional whispery sound of a mouse slipping through grass. There were crows. There were, however, no squirrels.

By midday Toaff had made himself a comfortable nest in the safety of the new den and he had located a pinecone to carry up with him and eat as he sat on a strong branch, watching the afternoon activity at the nest-house.

There was a lot of activity to watch.

Missus and the baby, with Sadie, went together into a

little field behind the poles and sat down, out of sight. Mister and Angus returned to the garbage. Mister held pieces of wood close together, then waved a front leg at them with short *thwap* sounds, *thwappety-thwap-thwappety*. Mister talked while he *thwap*ped and every now and then Angus yarked, "Yes," but Toaff had no idea what they were discussing. Besides, he was more interested in seeing the way Mister was turning the boards into another nest-house. A nest-house for garbage? Apparently it was, and it was just tall enough so that they could stand up in it. Mister put more boards on to make a top. Toaff couldn't imagine what Mister was thinking of, building a nest-house for something that wasn't alive.

By that time Missus and the baby and Sadie had returned to the nest-house. Mister said something to Angus. "Yes!" Angus agreed, his feathery tail sweeping across the ground.

Mister patted the top of the garbage-nest and then he lifted it, and dropped it, *crack!* He said something more to Angus.

"Yes!" Angus agreed again, and they went off together, back into the nest-house, where the voices of Missus and the baby, who was now saying *mah-mah-mah*, greeted them.

Toaff stayed hidden among the wispy needles of the fir and watched the day end. Mister brought the maybe-cows back to the nest-barn. Birds returned to their nests. The two cats slunk around the drive and the nest-barn and the pile of dirt. They even came up close to Toaff's tree, but they didn't seem aware that he was up there, sitting back on his haunches, looking down with his bright eyes at their long backs and thin tails. A cat could never catch a squirrel in a tree, he was sure of that now. Cats were too slow, they couldn't leap from branch to branch, and besides, even if a cat climbed up and trapped you on your branch, his balance wasn't good enough to allow him to attack, and he knew that even better than you did. Toaff was safe.

The golden air paled, turned purple and then gray and finally black. Mister took the dogs to the nest-barn. A *muuh-muuh*ing welcomed them, but then Mister came out, alone, and returned to the nest-house. After a while, the nest-house settled into silence. The sounds of insects faded away. A wind blew quietly through the trees in the woods and across the fields, and Toaff curled up in his nest.

# RACCOONS! IN THE GARDEN!

When the voices woke him that night, he crept out to listen. The raccoons were quarreling in front of the new garbage-nest. When raccoons quarreled, there was a lot of growling in the words. They sounded almost like angry dogs.

"There's nothing good in a garden yet. Let's just go on up to the lake."

"I say we try the garden first. Remember those tomatoes last fall? Okay, maybe a tomato doesn't fill your belly like a fish will, Rec, but most of us don't have bellies the size of yours. *Woo-hah.*"

"I'll open *your* belly, Rimble—"

"That'll do!" This was a new and bossy voice, a voice that expected to be obeyed. "Moon'll be full night after next and that's when we go up to the lake. No sooner and no later and no more discussion."

"Yessir, Cap'n," the two quarreling voices said.

"Even if we get that top off, there's still the covers," said Cap'n.

"He's got us this time," a fourth voice answered.

Cap'n said, "What's wood can be chewed through,

if you've got teeth. And I've got teeth. We'll test it when we return for winter. Tonight, it's the garden. And keep it down, boys. I don't want those dogs after me in the garden. Not with just the one hole in that fence."

Four low dark figures humped along toward that row of poles. They didn't return to the garbage, although Toaff hoped they would, and waited well into the moonlit night in that hope. He was wondering about that garden, which had to be the place behind the poles where Missus and Sadie and the baby had disappeared. If raccoons could forage there, so could a squirrel, maybe. But not in daytime. In daytime, the cats were always stalking—Fox alone, Snake alone, Fox and Snake side by side, Fox right behind Snake, Snake right behind Fox. . . . Didn't cats ever stop hunting?

He wondered—of course he did—if he shouldn't return to the horse chestnut tree. He could do that, he knew, and maybe he would. But he also wondered what the garden offered that the raccoons had been so eager to have. Tomatoes? What might tomatoes be? He'd never even heard of them. He might discover some food no squirrel before him had ever eaten. He liked the idea of being the first squirrel to discover something. He wondered if he dared to go into the garden at night.

Of course he did. Didn't he?

That was how it happened that on his third night alone, while the whole farm—except for one gray squirrel—was silent and sleeping, Toaff made his way down the trunk of the fir. Tail high, he dashed across to the nearest of the

150

poles that marked the edge of the garden. There, he found another thin wire wall, but this one had holes large enough for a squirrel to squeeze through onto soft dirt, and there he was—in the garden.

Before he wandered off from the protection of the wall, Toaff sat up on his haunches and looked around. Bright moonlight sucked the color out of everything, leaving just silvery grays and sharp blacks. Little grassy shoots were growing in straight lines, casting tiny dark shadows onto the bumpy ground. Everything was still, and silent, so Toaff left the wall and walked slowly along a row of shoots, keeping alert to any change in the air. From the center of the garden he could see that the poles carried their wall all the way around. Humans liked walls, he decided, stone walls or these wire-and-pole walls, and even the sides on their nests were high wooden walls. He wondered what was on top of those poles and decided to climb up one after he had eaten.

But squirrels didn't eat green chewy things, or even leafy things, and green, chewy, leafy things were all Toaff could find. Raccoons had different eating habits from squirrels, he decided. He turned to make his way across the moonlit garden back to the wire wall, and his fir. Maybe the leafy, chewy shoots were tomatoes, he thought, and wondered what garbage tasted like, since that was something else raccoons ate. That was the moment he heard them.

At first they were a low murmur of voices from the side of the garden farthest from the nest-house. It was Cap'n he heard, *chip*ping his words clearly. "It's right here, boys, we'll get ourselves some nice spinach or—"

Silence.

A listening, sniffing, stalking silence.

Toaff started to have a bad, nervous feeling. It ran up and down his legs and he checked to see where the nearest tree was. But there were no trees nearby, just the poles, and those poles had no branches.

"You smell that, Rad?" Rimble asked.

"Squirrel," Rad answered. "You think it's squirrel, Cap'n?"

"I think. And close," Cap'n answered. "Keep it low, boys, we don't want the dogs. . . ."

"I never want the dogs, *woo-hah*," said Rec, but in a low, whispery voice.

"Over there," said Rad.

Toaff bolted. Across rough dirt, not trying to avoid the shoots. The shoots would have to look out for themselves, he thought, setting his paws right on them to leap up onto one of the poles and dig his nails in to scramble up to the top. The top was flat! He was standing on something flat, and round, and not very high off the ground. High *enough* off the ground? he wondered.

"Up there, Cap'n," Rimble murmured. "Want me to get him?"

"You go up, we'll surround the pole," Rad answered. Then he added, "That's your plan, isn't it, Cap'n?"

"That's it," Cap'n said. "We've got him trapped."

Trapped? The four dark humped shapes had gathered right below him, and they sounded sure that he was trapped. Toaff didn't *feel* trapped, but if he couldn't go down to the ground, because that was where they were, and they could get up to where he was, what else was he but trapped?

Toaff looked down at the dark shapes and tried to think, but all he wanted to do was run.

"Don't be frightened, little squirrel," Rec whispered up. "It'll all be over soon. Up you go, Rimble."

One raccoon wrapped his legs around the pole and started to climb.

Toaff looked around, looked everywhere. Rimble was a slow enough climber that Toaff had time to scramble down, except that they had the pole surrounded and he knew he wouldn't have time to get himself through one of the holes before—

He gathered his feet under him, getting ready, because hopeless or not, he'd have to move. Except not down, and there was no more up.

He looked across at the next of the garden poles. He couldn't be sure in the untrustworthy moonlight, but maybe he had a chance. If he didn't have that chance, he didn't have any chance at all. *Do I have to—?*

Toaff leaped. He leaped up and out, the empty dark air beneath him. He leaped across . . . and he landed! Safe on the top of the next pole! If there hadn't been raccoons on the ground below, he would have whuffled, whuffling at their surprised grunts, whuffling at his escape. Whuffling

153

for happiness, a sudden and entirely unexpected happiness. Because even though Rimble jumped easily down and the raccoons were now lumbering after him, Toaff had an idea. He knew what to do.

"*Chuk-chuk-chuk,*" he screeched as loudly as he could. "*Chuk-chuk!*"

"What's he—?"

"Stop him!" Cap'n whispered hoarsely.

The raccoons gathered together, but not around Toaff's pole.

"*Chuk-chuk-chuk!*" he screeched, and a dog answered him from the nest-barn. "What?" it yarked, once, sharply, then fell silent. All of the creatures in the garden knew it was listening.

Toaff waited. Raccoons were wild creatures, like squirrels, and he didn't want the dogs to get them. Not as much as he didn't want the raccoons to get *him*, but enough to give them a choice.

"He's like that Fredle," Rimble complained, but still whispering. "Think it's his brother?"

"Fredle wasn't a squirrel, dumbhead," Rec answered.

"You think I didn't know that? You're the dumbhead," Rimble said.

"Anyway," Cap'n announced in a low voice. "We can't drive him down. That's clear."

"We could outwait him," Rad suggested. "Make him go from pole to pole until he's tired, and he falls, and we get him."

Cap'n wasn't convinced. "And give him time to make another ruckus? It'll be daylight before he gets tired. Didn't you see him? He jumps easy as some bird."

The dogs yarked again, Sadie asking, "Is somebody out there?" and Angus joining in, "I see you!"

They were all silent, the squirrel to give the raccoons a chance, the dogs to know if they had really heard something, the raccoons to be sure it was safe. After a very long time, "All right, boys," Cap'n said, and he sounded tired. "Let's be on our way. Tomorrow's the day."

"You heard him." Rad repeated the orders in a cheerful voice, and concluded, "Tomorrow's the day. Tomorrow, the Rowdy Boys go back to the lake. There's fish waiting in the lake for us, and fish's better than squirrel any day."

Toaff almost trembled himself off his pole, in his relief. But he didn't. He waited, shivering, until they were gone, and then he waited a lot longer, until the thick, sleeping silence of night convinced him he could descend, and return safely to his own safe den.

# INTRODUCING SADIE

After that, Toaff stuck close to home. On long, hot summer days and during the warm summer rains, he chewed away at the fir and carried in more mouthfuls of grasses and leaves, until he had made himself a comfortable nest in a den that was now big enough for a full-grown squirrel and his winter stores. That done, he then discovered that there was good foraging everywhere on this side of the nest-house. The pile of dirt turned out to be filled with food, and so was the area where the dogs ate every morning, spilling brown things and water. The crows' *kaah-kaah*ing had called his attention to both of those places, probably saying *Food here!* but whether telling one another or for the benefit of a nearby squirrel, Toaff didn't know. What he did know was that from the pile to his tree was an easy run, and that he could escape to safety behind the wooden wall-with-holes, if he had to. He could stand the stink of mouse, if it was a matter of life or death. His life or his death. It turned out that he didn't care if the crows meant him to know about the food; the important thing was to know that food was to be found in those places.

The garden also was a safe place to be, in daylight. The cats seemed uninterested in it, Missus and the baby were the only humans who went there, and the one animal was Sadie. Even though there was no food of real interest to him in the garden, he liked to perch on a pole and watch the comings and goings of humans and animals and machines at the nest-house and nest-barn.

It was probably inevitable that he'd be noticed. And it was not surprising at all that it was Sadie who first saw him.

That morning Sadie was yarking "Goodbye! Good luck!" to Angus and Mister, who were being taken down the driveway by a machine. "Goodbye! Goodbye!" Sadie called as she ran after the machine. When it got away, she ran back up the drive. That was when she saw Toaff.

She had caught him going into the garden, so he fled up a pole. Perched safely on its top, he waved his tail and chittered down fiercely, to persuade her to be afraid of him, or at least to leave him alone, or maybe to just stop her yarking.

She couldn't understand what he was saying. "What? What?" she yarked. Then she sat down, and dragged her tail back and forth through the wet grass. "It rained!" she told him.

"I know," Toaff answered.

"What?" she asked. "Angus *yarkyark* ribbon. Angus *yark* get a leg."

"Did he lose one of his legs?" Toaff asked. This was an amazing piece of news, and an alarming possibility. "I didn't see a missing leg."

"What?" Sadie said. "You aren't a dog," she told him.

"I know," said Toaff.

"Or a cat."

"I'm a squirrel."

"What?" Sadie yarked. "What are you saying? I'm a dog," she told him. "I don't think you're a mouse? Are you? I think you're a squirrel."

Toaff started to whuffle. He couldn't help it.

"Are you all right?" Sadie asked, and now she stood up on her hind legs, almost as tall as the pole, and her black nose was much too close, and her long teeth, too.

Toaff gathered his legs under him and leaped, through the air to the next pole.

"Look at you!" yarked Sadie. She ran after him, but he was too quick for her. "Play!" she yarked happily. "Play!"

Toaff was glad to do just that. There was a lot of only in Sadie, he decided. It was too bad she was a dog.

Not many days later, Missus also noticed Toaff, who was on top of a pole, waiting for the chance to run to safety. She said something to Sadie, who was busy helping the baby move through the garden dirt by pushing it with her nose. Sadie answered, "Maybe squirrel?" and Missus said something else, to which Sadie said, "Baby safe." But Missus kept on watching Toaff and he was worried about what that watching meant.

After a while, Sadie came closer to his pole, dragging the baby, who was holding on to her tail with its paws. "Squirrel?" she yarked.

"Yes," Toaff answered softly, since he wondered if a quieter voice might help her understand. "Yes, squirrel." He used as few words as possible. "Toaff."

"What?" Sadie yarked loudly. "What?"

Missus looked up, watching again.

Everything was quiet, just for a few heartbeats, and in that quiet time, it was Sadie who heard the voice first. She turned her head to point her ears toward the stone wall that separated the garden from the woods beyond. Then Toaff heard it, too, and he understood what it was saying.

It was saying his name. "Toaff? Toaff?"

Sadie jerked her tail free and ran yarking back to the end of the garden nearest the wall. Missus came to pick up the baby, but Toaff no longer cared about them. The voice was chukking his name, so it had to be a squirrel, and not just any squirrel: *Gray* squirrels were the ones who chukked.

# INTRODUCING THE LITTLES

Toaff scampered down the pole to run outside the garden, around to that wall. Standing on top of a stone, he listened some more, and sniffed. At first he heard just the wind brushing through pine branches and whispering in the leaves of trees. He smelled only pine trees and dirt. He saw just trunks and pine branches and low bushes. Then he heard faint murmuring sounds, like squirrels speaking in their smallest voices, squirrels who were afraid to be heard or seen. Slowly, carefully, he moved over the stones toward those voices. When he came close enough to understand them, a voice no louder than falling snow said, "I must have been wrong."

"Yes." A soft, sad agreement.

"What will we do now?" An unhappy question.

Toaff didn't know what to do. He didn't want to frighten them. He wondered if he should whisper, too, or maybe he should just reassure them in his normal voice, *Don't worry, it's safe enough here.* He took two more steps and he still couldn't see them. Where were they?

"Hello?" he called softly.

There was a brief silence, then the first voice answered. "Hello?"

"I can't see you," Toaff said.

"We're hiding," the voice answered.

"You found a good place to hide in," Toaff said. What was going on? Normally, at the sound of another squirrel's friendly voice, a gray squirrel would come popping out.

"*I* found it!" announced a second voice. "It was me!"

Toaff felt like whuffling, but he didn't. "That was a good job of finding you did," he said, trying to sound serious, and he followed the trail of voices a few more steps along the top of the wall.

"I tried," claimed a third. "I tried hard. I tried as hard as I could, didn't I, Leaf?"

Leaf was the first voice, and it responded, "You did. We all tried, and Neef was the best finder this time."

"Or maybe that's me!" Toaff announced as he jumped down to the ground. He stood right in front of the piled-up stones, but not close enough to block an opening and not until he had looked all around to be sure there wasn't any danger nearby. Toaff hoped that he would be safe, for a little time at least, out in the open like that.

The furry face of a gray squirrel appeared in an opening and asked, "Toaff?"

Huddled beside her, but still hidden back in the darkness, were two more squirrels, but all Toaff could see of them was four shiny black eyes.

"Yes, hello, are you Leaf?" he asked.

"Hello, yes, I'm Leaf, how did you know?" She answered herself, "Tief said it, didn't he?" As she spoke, she emerged from the stones, a small gray squirrel whose tail was not nearly as fat with fur as it would be when she was full grown. "Come out, you two. It's safe," she said. "I think."

"It is," Toaff said as two equally small gray squirrels came hesitantly out.

"We're still little," the smallest said. Then he told Toaff, "I'm Neef."

Leaf introduced the other one. "And this is Tief."

"You really are little," Toaff realized.

"Too little to be on our own," Tief agreed. "And I wish we weren't because I want my mother. I know I'm not supposed to say that anymore, but I do. I really do." He turned to Leaf. "I'm sorry."

Leaf explained. "We were moving to a better territory, running through the grass, and I think it took longer than our mother thought it would, because—"

"There was a wind, or it was like a wind, and then she was going up into the air like—" Neef interrupted.

"And she screamed," Tief added, in a small voice.

"Then she stopped screaming," Neef said.

"A hawk, I think," Leaf concluded. "The wings were *dark*, like the wind at night—and she was gone. So we're trying to find the better territory by ourselves."

They were all silent, looking at one another, until finally Tief couldn't stand it any longer. "Will you take us with you? Please? Toaff? It's so big out here, and I'm little," he said, in a complaining-explaining voice. "You have a nest, don't you?"

"It's not very large," Toaff said.

"We don't mind," Leaf told him. "We can help make it bigger. If you let us. I can forage, too. We can be quiet."

Toaff had already made up his mind. These Littles needed time to learn how to take care of themselves. He could show them what he knew, about building nests and dreys and dens, about predators, about places to forage. He knew the safety rules, too, because he had already been outside for weeks before *his* mother went away. He could help them.

Also, he wanted to take them to his den. It would be crowded, but he'd like to sleep in a den crowded with warm furry bodies, for a change. "Follow me," he said, and hurried off along the stone wall path back to his fir.

As soon as the Littles were inside, they crowded into Toaff's small nest and fell asleep, all of them piled up together, without saying a word. It happened in three blinks of an eye and then there Toaff was, looking into his own den from outside, as if he was the stranger and they were the ones who belonged. He whuffled quietly at the surprises any day might bring with it. But he knew it wouldn't be long before hunger overcame exhaustion, so he searched out a pinecone large enough to provide food for all of them and carried it back to the entrance. There, he sat on a branch and waited for the Littles to wake up.

The Littles were awake just long enough to pick everything edible out of the pinecone and then fall asleep again.

But not before Leaf thanked
Toaff. "I knew you could
help, I knew you would, because we're so new and little."

"I'm not that big,"
Toaff told her. He hadn't
come out until the winter,
after all.

"Not like us," Leaf said.
"Not like us, we're new-little and you're old-little and . . ."
She was asleep before she could finish that thought. All
the rest of the afternoon, Toaff waited and waited for them
to wake up. But they had had a long and difficult journey
and they didn't stir, so eventually, when it grew dark, Toaff
crawled onto the top of the pile of squirrels stuffed into his
nest, to fall asleep himself.

# 32

## DOG TALES AND SHEEP STORIES

In the morning the Littles burst into life. Maybe it was because, as usual, the dogs ran up to the nest-house yarking so they were startled awake, and when they tried to move, their legs and tails got all tangled up, which made them whuffle wildly. Maybe it was the good night's sleep after a long, hard journey. Whatever the reason, the Littles were full of energy and the need to run and chitter. Leaf jumped up onto the branch where Toaff sat watching Angus and Sadie eat, to tell him, "Those are the dogs."

"I know," Toaff said.

"The sheep tell them things," Leaf informed him.

*What do you know about sheep?* Toaff wanted to ask, but Leaf kept on explaining.

"We can't understand much of what the dogs say but I know their names, Ang and Say. Our mother told us that. Our mother could understand a lot of what the sheep told the dogs to tell us."

Toaff would have told her the dogs' whole names, but Leaf continued to explain.

"Sheep know squirrels can't understand them."

Toaff knew from Braff where the sheep were to be found and he wondered if she had seen Braff, and maybe Soaff, too. "Did you come from behind the nest-barn?" he asked.

Leaf swung around to look right at him. Her round black eyes glistened brightly and her tail waved in excitement. "Behind the nest-barn is where we want to go! That's where the sheep said to go!"

"Then why were you at the garden?" he asked, confused.

"Garden?" Leaf asked, and now she was confused too. But right then was when Tief and Neef came scrambling up to ask, "Is there another pinecone? I'm hungry, aren't you? Can you find us some food, Toaff?" And since they were all having a big morning hunger, the four squirrels went to forage together. Toaff showed them how seeds could be found in the grass by the stone wall, and cones near the firs, and all kinds of food in the dirt pile. It wasn't until they had all crowded back into the nest that night that Toaff had a chance to ask his questions.

A squirrel had to be very tired to fall asleep jammed up with three other squirrels in a nest built for one. Neef and Tief could do it right away but Toaff and Leaf were wakeful. So they talked in low voices, in the sleeping darkness of night on the farm, when only the wind was still awake and restless, the wind and those creatures who hunt by night.

Leaf knew she was a guest and wanted to apologize. "I'm sorry that this fir trunk is too narrow for us to chew more room for a bigger den."

166

Toaff's head was jammed up against hard wood but he wanted to be polite. "We'll find another nest for you to-morrow. There's sure to be a good place for a den for you in the woods."

"But we don't know—" Leaf began, and then she stopped herself. Toaff felt her shift in the darkness. He could almost *feel* her, staring at the dark shape that was him. He could almost *hear* her thinking.

Then, as if Toaff hadn't said anything about the Littles moving out of his nest, Leaf started talking again. "It was the lake that came first, of the whole farm. Did you know that? The sheep made the lake first. Do you know how they made the lake? Do you know what a lake is?"

"It's a big puddle, isn't it?"

"It's water," she said, again as if he hadn't spoken. "It's a whole wide field of water that stretches from one hillside to another and is so big it never disappears, all year long. It ripples when the wind blows over it, and when no wind blows, it lies smooth and still as the sky. If you fall into the lake, you sink and sink and never come to its bottom, and you're never seen again because the lake takes you. The same way as when a hawk comes out of the sky to take you up and up until you disappear."

Toaff asked, "Does the lake hunt squirrels?"

Leaf whuffled softly. "No. The lake isn't like that, the lake is a good thing. That's why the sheep made it, so there will always be water. They made the lake first and then the little streams. I've never seen the lake but others have, and

167

everyone knows why the sheep wanted to make it, and how they made it. And I've seen a stream so I know the lake is real, somewhere. Do you want to hear how the sheep made it?"

She wanted to tell him the story, so Toaff didn't interrupt again.

"At first," Leaf said, "there was the farm with its fields, and the grasses and trees, and the wild animals in the woods, and that was all. But the sheep knew that animals need water and so do the grasses and trees. So they chose a good place, a wide meadow up in the hills, and they began to eat all the grass there. They ate and they ate. Day after day they ate as much as they could, until that whole wide meadow was bare dirt. Then they began to run on the dirt, back and forth and around, stamping down hard on the ground, until it sank away under their hooves. When it had sunk away so far that no sheep could see how deep it was, they all went back up the hillside and waited."

Leaf fell silent, as if she was one of those sheep, waiting.

Finally Toaff asked, "Waited for what?"

"Waited until the moon was full. On that night they all gathered together to sing their water song. The sheep knew that when the moon is full, the water underground comes up close to the surface, to catch some of the moon's silver. So on that full moon night, they sang their song. *Bau-bau* is all our ears can hear, so we don't know the song."

Toaff had heard *bau-bau*ing; he knew that sound.

Leaf continued. "But the oldest things do know that song, the water and the wind and the rocks underground.

*Bau-bau*, sang the sheep, and the water came closer, to hear. *Bau-bau*, they sang, until the water broke up, up through the dirt and rocks at the bottom of the deep deep meadow. The sheep kept singing, and the water kept rising up to hear their song, until the lake was filled with water, enough for fish to swim in and enough for the little streams to take with them when they ran away down the hillside carrying water to all the creatures they passed on their way, and all the grasses and trees, too."

Leaf stopped again, and waited again, until Toaff spoke.

"That's a good story," he said. "What did the crows have to say about the lake?"

"Crows don't say things. Just sheep. And dogs, and us."

"What about humans?" Toaff asked. "Did they want the lake?"

"It was before the sheep brought the humans to the farm, but that's too long a story for tonight," Leaf answered. "I'm too tired to tell it now. Tomorrow, Toaff, can you wait until tomorrow?"

If he had to, Toaff could wait, and so he agreed.

# GUESTS WHO WILL
# NOT GO AWAY

The next day, whenever Toaff suggested that maybe the Littles wanted to find themselves a larger den, Leaf explained, "We don't need another den because the sheep want us to go behind the nest-barn. That's what the dogs said."

That evening, Leaf announced, "Toaff wants to hear how the humans came to the farm. Do you want to hear that story again?"

"Yes," Neef said, and Tief said, "Yes, please." They shifted in the nest, making themselves more comfortable, to listen.

Toaff's head was jammed up against the top of the den again. He hadn't asked about any story and he started to insist, gently and politely, but firmly, that tomorrow the Littles had to go. "I'm sorry—" he began, but Leaf had started talking.

"The sheep had the lake, for water. They had the trees, for shelter. But sheep need to eat, and with the meadow gone they had just the sparse grasses at the edges of the woods. Each morning the sheep woke up hungrier than the day before, and they wandered around like lost things until the youngest ram had a new idea. It's the young who have more ideas, even if they don't know enough to tell the good ones from the bad. Luckily, this was a good one. 'Humans,' he said. 'We need humans to cut down the trees and make pastures for us, and we'll let them live on the farm as long as they take proper care of us.'

"What the young ram had not thought of," Leaf continued, "which others did, was how hard it is to capture a human. But one of the oldest rams had a good idea, because when the old *do* have ideas, they are often good ones. The old ram said, 'We'll go to the road, and when a machine comes along, we'll take its human.'"

Toaff knew about the road. He told them, "Machines go on the road. Machines are really dangerous." He was about to announce that this story couldn't possibly be true, but Leaf interrupted.

"The sheep knew that," Leaf said. "But they had to have a human even if everyone knows those machines squish and squash and then just keep going as if they can't even feel what they've done. But one of the mothers—she had a lamb to care for and feed—argued that there was no other good idea to try. 'A sheep is smart enough to figure out how to stop a machine,' she said. 'We just need one human,' she said. So the sheep found a stream to follow down to the road. While they were traveling, they had to eat whatever they could find in the woods. They ate pine needles and fallen-down dried-up leaves and it was a very hard journey."

At that point in her story, Leaf fell silent, and listened. "Sleeping," she announced to Toaff, "and I think I will too, now that everything is quiet."

"But," he protested, "you didn't say how they got their human. You never told me what sheep look like."

"Oh," she said in a sleepy voice. "Like dogs. But bigger, and they have thick thick curly hair. Like deer, with their thin thin legs."

"I don't know what a deer looks like," he protested. "Don't go to sleep yet."

"Like a dog but bigger, but with longer thinner legs and not much of a tail and no hair and . . ." Leaf slid into the night's slumbers.

# LEAF EXPLAINS EVERYTHING

Toaff knew perfectly well what Leaf was doing. As long as there was a story he wouldn't get to hear if they moved out of his den, he wasn't going to make them leave. Toaff knew that and—actually?—he didn't mind. He was a squirrel and squirrels love stories.

Also, like any squirrel, Toaff was just as happy to be with others as to be alone. Except for the overcrowded nest at night, he enjoyed having the Littles around—the games, the conversations, the foraging together and sharing what they found to eat. He especially liked the way they listened to him when he told them where food might be found and taught them about keeping safe from the cats. Toaff was the one who knew things. Being the one who knew was a new way of being only, and he liked it.

So the stories continued, and the Littles stayed on. Toaff heard how, when one machine after another had simply swerved around a sheep that stood right out on the road, the herd determined on a bold and dangerous move. Instead of depending on one sheep, who was usually young and male, to have the courage to face one of those machines, they decided to leave mothers and lambs behind while all the others, ewes and rams, old and young, clustered together on the road. Clustered together they took up so much of the road that the machine couldn't swerve by, and had to stop, and then, when its human had herded them—which was what he thought he was doing—out of his way, they led him up the drive to where a nest-house waited. Once he had come as far as the nest-house, he stayed on, just as they had planned. He cleared the woods, sometimes to make a pasture for the sheep and sometimes to make a field where he could grow winter food for them. After that, the human ran the farm to serve the sheep. This had all happened long, long ago, so long ago no sheep could remember it for himself.

When Toaff asked, "What about the dogs?" Leaf knew the story, but he had to wait for the next night to hear it.

It was hard for humans to understand what sheep wanted, she pointed out. So the sheep asked for dogs, to be their messengers, their translators and special servants. When Toaff asked, "What about squirrels?" she reminded him that the uneaten seeds and nuts buried and forgotten by squirrels became more trees, to provide shelter for the humans who took care of the sheep. When he wondered next about cats, and raccoons and foxes, and raptors, too, the owls and hawks, she whuffled. "You forgot eagles. They're the strongest of all the birds. Never forget eagles. But didn't you ever think how crowded with squirrels the woods would be if there were no predators? Squirrels would have babies and those babies would have more babies and all of those squirrels would eat all of the seeds and nuts, and where would the new trees come from? Humans need trees and humans serve the sheep, so the sheep want just a certain number of squirrels. They send predators to take care of the rest."

Eventually Toaff heard how the Littles came to be hiding in the garden wall that day. "You can smell fall just coming here," Leaf said, "but in the mountains it had already arrived, and when the dogs came to find out what the sheep wanted, the sheep told the dogs to announce, *Behind the nest-barn!*"

"But I thought you couldn't understand what the dogs say," Toaff pointed out.

"We worked it out," Leaf told him. "We talked about it and figured it out all together."

"I heard *nest-barn*," Neef boasted. "Everybody heard it. And so did I!"

"Squirrels knew *nest-barn* already," Tief assured Toaff. "But it took our mother to figure out *behind*."

Leaf explained, "It's never easy to be sure exactly what the sheep want the dogs to tell us. It's hard to understand exactly what the dogs are saying, because they yark and sturf so much. But the squirrels have learned a few words. *Play* and *nest-barn* are two words the dogs say over and over and we know for sure that we know them."

"We know *obey*, too," Neef added, "and *here*."

Leaf said, "Some squirrels heard *hind* and some argued

that it was *be*. They quarreled about that until someone asked, 'Could it be both?' But *hindbe* made no sense. *Nest-barn hindbe?* Or *hindbe nest-barn?* Everyone was guessing, and each everyone said he had it right."

"It was our mother who really did get it right," Tief announced proudly. "Even though no one had asked her what she thought, our mother said *behind*."

"Which made sense," Neef pointed out. "It was our mother who made sense."

"So even if it's not always easy to know what the sheep want us to do," Leaf concluded, "that time we did."

Having realized what the sheep wanted them to do, the squirrels began their journey. *Nest-barn* had to do with the human, they guessed, so the place to look first was the nest-house. The nest-house, they had heard, was no more than four days' journey if you found the stream and followed it. But it was hard to find the stream, and there had been no shelter along the way, so one after the other, most of the squirrels were picked off, by foxes and fishers and owls.

This was the third time he'd heard the word, but before Toaff could ask about *fisher*, "We hid from the raccoons," Neef told him. "They never even knew we were there."

"They were talking about the lake, but I don't think sheep want raccoons near their lake, do you? Raccoons are so dirty and rough, and they eat almost anything, and they try to steal our babies when the mothers aren't there to protect them. Raccoons are—"

"We don't have to worry about raccoons coming here,"

Leaf said soothingly, and Toaff did not bother to correct her. He had a different concern.

"If the sheep wanted you to go behind the nest-barn, why did so many squirrels get hunted down?"

"I think there were too many of us, many too many, so the others had to die. I think it's just us little ones who are supposed to be behind the nest-barn, and I think we're supposed to wait there for the sheep," Leaf answered him. "I thought about it all and that's the one thing that makes sense. Because," she reminded him, "the sheep take care of us. They know we can't understand them, so they ask the dogs to tell us what they want us to do, and that's what the dogs said."

"What about the humans?" Toaff asked, remembering what the Lucky Ones thought.

"Humans are nothing to do with squirrels," Leaf told him. "They're here to take care of the sheep. The sheep take care of everything else, squirrels, raccoons, dogs, probably even cats, too, if we could know what sheep think."

"What about birds?"

"Hawks and owls? Their job is to hunt us."

"I mean crows."

She thought for a minute. "I think crows must have been a mistake, don't you? They don't help the sheep and they don't do anything useful either."

"What about snowstorms, or windstorms? Or rainstorms when the sky explodes with that sharp light?" If Leaf could just see one little crack in what she was saying, then maybe she would see that the rest didn't make sense, not really.

Unless it *did* make sense and it was Toaff who just couldn't see it?

"Is rain the same as rainstorm?" Leaf asked.

# IN THE DEN, IN A SUMMER STORM

Two days later, her question was answered. A strong wind rose. It blew itself in, in the dark of night, to push against and pull at their fir, pushing against the trunk and pulling at the branches, trying, and trying again, to force the tree down onto its side and rip its roots out of the ground. The wind brought a beating rain that came down so fast and heavy that no squirrel dared to put even his nose out into the stormy day, lest he be washed out of his den, and blown away, and lost.

All that night, their young fir swayed, back and forth, from side to side. The wind swirled around its trunk and the rain washed down on its needles. All through that dark night and all through the next day, too—a day that stayed as dim as dawn—the wind whistled and the rain lashed and the fir bent easily and swung gently back upright and Toaff didn't worry.

However, as the storm pounded the fir hour after hour after hour, Toaff began to think about the big drey, so high up in its maple. Was it built strongly enough to withstand such a storm? Was it securely enough placed on its branches? He remembered how thick its walls were and the way it nestled down into three strong, thick branches. Probably the Lucky Ones were safe, he hoped.

The four squirrels in Toaff's small den huddled uncomfortably together. All they could do was talk, about sheep and dogs, raccoons and birds, the lake, the apple trees, the pasture. Toaff told them about his first nest, with Braff and Soaff, Old Criff, his mother, and the others, in the big den in the dead pine tree near the horse chestnut. He made an exciting story out of the winter snowstorm and waking up alone, about Mister and the chain saw and his flight to the apple trees. Until he told it as stories, he didn't realize how interesting his life so far had been.

The storm continued, into the next night, and eventually even stories couldn't keep the Littles from being uneasy and afraid. It was Tief who spoke up, in a small voice, and admitted, "I don't like it when our nest moves like this."

Neef burst out with a question he couldn't hold in any longer. "Is our tree going to blow over too? Will it hurt?"

Then Leaf said, "You know, we're not doing what the sheep told us. Maybe the sheep sent the storm to remind us," she suggested. "They told us, *Behind the nest-barn.* That's what the dogs said."

"They did. They did," agreed Tief and Neef, and for some reason, maybe because Leaf had brought the two ideas so close together, that was when Toaff finally remembered something Braff had told him.

"Do the sheep go behind the nest-barn in winter?" he asked.

Nobody could tell him. They hadn't come outside until summer.

"Because," Toaff explained, "when my littermate came back after—before Mister and the chain saw but after the tree blew down—"

"Don't talk about that!"

"Braff told me they had gone where the sheep were. He said the humans fed the sheep."

"Of course they do, if there's no pasture. Didn't you listen to what I told you? That's why the sheep have humans here on the farm." Leaf shifted around until her head was close to Toaff's. "Do you know the way to the nest-barn?"

At that, Toaff whuffled so loudly even the wind couldn't drown it out.

She drew back as far as she could in that small space. "You shouldn't laugh. Not when it's something the sheep told us."

Toaff tried to point out, "It was the dogs who told you."

"That's their job. The sheep tell the dogs so the dogs can tell us."

"When this storm stops, after we eat, I'll show you the nest-barn," Toaff promised.

"When *will* it stop?" wailed Neef.

"Storms stop when they stop and not before," Toaff told him. "But they do stop. *That* I'm sure of."

"Really sure?" Tief asked.

"Really sure," Toaff promised, and of course he was right.

# FALL

# TOAFF CHANGES HIS MIND

After a night and a day and another night of wild wind and slashing rain, the storm went on to bother another farm and a sunny morning dawned over the farm. The four squirrels burst out of the small den to breathe in the warm summer air. But the air wasn't warm. It had been rinsed in coldness before it came out to fill the sky. It was crisp and it tasted fresher than any air Toaff had breathed since early spring. It was also full of busy sounds, machine sounds and human sounds and a faint smell of—was it apples? The dogs yarked excitedly and the chain saw screeched. Crows *kaah-kaah*ed their way across the sky and the cows *muuh-muuh*ed, but these voices sounded quick and hurrying, not slow and lazy. In this cool morning weather, all the voices sounded sharper.

Toaff guessed that fall had begun and he knew he was right even if he didn't know how he knew. Fall made him hungry, and full of strength, as if he could leap and run all the way to the front of the nest-house and back around to his fir and no cat could catch him.

However, all of this noisy activity made the Littles uneasy and unhappy. They ran right back to the den as soon as they had eaten and huddled there until hunger drove them out to forage again. When the farm was just as busy the next morning, Leaf made up their minds.

"We want to go to behind the nest-barn," she announced. "Right now. We can forage when we get there. Where is the nest-barn, Toaff? Do you know?"

"It's right there. Beyond the garden," Toaff answered.

"Isn't that a nest?"

"No, it's the nest-barn," Toaff said. Then he wondered if he could be sure his word for it was righter than any other, and added, "I think."

"I see it," Leaf said, but she had something else to wonder about. "I also see two cats and I see one of those machines that carry humans." She meant to say that she saw danger without using that exact word in front of Neef and Tief. "But you know a safe-path," she told Toaff.

"I'm not going with you," he told her. He was thinking of apples, remembering the two small trees.

"You have to!" they all cried, all of their six black eyes bright with alarm. "Why would you stay here when the dog told us about you so you *know* the sheep want you to come with us?"

"What dog told you about me?"

"Say did. When we were hiding," Neef said.

"Say told us your name so we could call you. Don't you remember?" asked Tief.

"Can we go *now?*" Leaf asked him. "Right away? Because if we don't, the sheep might send another storm."

"We better go," the others echoed. "We're not supposed to stay here."

"Toaff?" Leaf asked, and said, without saying the words, *You're the one who knows the way so you have to, please.*

Toaff was getting a little tired of being the one who knew things, and also he had never actually been anywhere close to the nest-barn, so he *didn't* know any way. He was about to say his goodbyes to the Littles when the dogs came yarking out of the nest-house, with Mister right behind them. "Come on, Sadie, the sheep *yarkyark!*" Angus said, and Sadie answered, "Herd sheep! Run! Crouch!" Then Mister said something short and sharp and they all jumped up into one of the machines and it went along the drive, but not toward the road. It went away from the nest-house and nest-barn in the other direction.

"Did you hear? Say said *sheep!*" Leaf cried.

"So did Ang!" Neef cried. "We have to go!"

"We're already late!" Tief cried.

"Toaff?" Leaf asked again, with even more *please* in her voice.

"You go," Toaff said. "I'm staying," and before they could argue, or begin another story, he scrambled down the trunk of the fir. He ran along the stone wall, heading for the garbage-nest and the bushes and eventually the apple trees. But as soon as he came to the drive, he had to stop. And stare.

Toaff stared at the disaster that had happened beside the big white nest-house. There was a pile of cut-up oak branches beside the garbage-nest and a confusion of long maple and oak branches lying on the grass. It looked as if the storm had grabbed those three tall trees and dug its nails in, and jerked. Jerked hard. Jerked hard, again and again. Then, when it had ripped off a branch, it lost interest and dropped the broken thing onto the grass before moving on to its next victim. The storm was like a cat hunting not for hunger but for its own amusement.

Peering up into the high branches of the first maple tree, Toaff caught sight of the drey, tilted badly to one side but still safe on its branches. So that was all right. Then he saw that two squirrels stared out over its edge toward the feeder, where— He *had* to dash across the drive to see what they were staring at— It was gray and furry and on the ground, half hidden among the leaves of a fallen branch.

The gray and furry thing was not moving.

Toaff couldn't move either. Snake and Fox were making a slow, stalking approach toward it. They hadn't noticed him and Toaff didn't want to find out what they had in mind for a squirrel who was already dead. He unfroze his legs and turned around, to head back.

When he moved, the two remaining Lucky Ones noticed him. "Look what you did to Tzaaf!" they called. "Just look!" they called after him as he dashed back across the drive.

Toaff would have liked to stop and tell them that he hadn't done anything to Tzaaf, that it was the storm that did it. He wanted to call back up to them that the storm wasn't any of his doing. It wasn't anything the humans did either, in his opinion, because look at all the broken branches, and humans liked the trees, otherwise wouldn't they cut them all down? *It's not my fault*, he would have liked to have told them, loud and clear, and he would have, if it hadn't been for the danger of cats and the sadness of that mound of gray fur.

Maybe he *would* go with the Littles, after all. Maybe he *should* finally do what Braff had told him, long ago at winter's end, even if it was bossy Braff who suggested it. Maybe, after all, it would be better to live behind the nest-barn with the Littles, and keep on being the one who had to know about things.

When he got back to the fir, Leaf greeted him happily. "I knew you'd help us. Say said."

All Toaff answered was "Let's go."

He wanted to be far from that drey, and far from humans, too.

# BEHIND THE NEST-BARN

They traveled in a line, with Toaff in the lead. They listened intently, all ears cocked. They looked as sharply as they could in all directions, to be sure no cats were on the prowl, and Toaff didn't tell them that he was pretty sure the cats were occupied elsewhere. They ran behind the high mound of dirt, then over to the garden.

In single file, with Toaff still first and Leaf at the rear, they dashed from pole to pole around the garden to the stone wall beyond it. After that, they moved through the branches and leaves the storm had tossed around, following the stone wall.

Then the chain saw screeched and the Littles scattered, squeezing into any available crack among the rocks. They really did need him, Toaff thought; he was the one who knew what was happening. He went from one quivering Little to the other, waiting for the chain saw to fall silent to explain quietly, "It's nothing to do with us. Mister's cutting up the branches that the wind blew down. He's going to take them away, like he did my dead pine. It's nothing to do with us. Remember what I told you about my dead pine? Mister's cutting up some big branches over by the nest-house. He's nowhere near here."

Eventually the journey resumed, until the stone wall reached the nest-barn wall, which loomed over them, and behind the nest-barn they found a small, grassy pasture. "We're here! This is behind the nest-barn! Is this behind the nest-barn, Toaff?"

Toaff considered the question. One side of the pasture was the high nest-barn wall but the three other sides were surrounded by wooden poles held apart by long pieces of bare branches. It would be easy for a squirrel to go in and out of the pasture. There were no animals in the pasture, but there *was* a small nest-house huddled up close to the nest-barn. Nothing was moving, not in the small nest-house or in the grassy pasture or in the woods that stretched away all around it. Except for the sound of the chain saw from far away, there was nothing to hear but the usual sounds of insects and the wind. "I think it is," he decided, adding, "Yes, it is." Because it had to be.

Toaff wondered why Braff and the others had left this place, and then he wondered if they had safely crossed the road. He saw how the woods were crowded with pines and firs and spruces, which meant plenty of pinecones for a squirrel's winter hoard. He looked for squirrels, for an entrance to a den, for a drey. He looked for places among the trees at the edges where a drey might be built, or to see the kind of hollow that might be the entrance to a den. He stood still, looking about and wondering.

The Littles were running around and calling out.

"Sheep were here!"

"Look! This is some of their fur. Look, Toaff!"

"It's sticking right on this pole!"

"Smell that, Toaff!"

Toaff sniffed. A faint odor hung in the air, something sharp and a little oily. It was unpleasant, so Toaff went back to considering the woods, ignoring the high voices of the Littles. He remembered that Braff had said the sheep stayed in something called a pen behind the nest-barn, which this certainly could be, since *pen* was a word with definite edges, just like this pasture.

Meanwhile, the Littles ran along from pole to pole, calling out to one another.

"Sheep fur!"

"It's everywhere!"

"We're here!"

"We did it!"

Toaff said nothing, but he stared into the woods, searching for a possible den, until—suddenly, unexpectedly, and entirely surprisingly—he knew exactly where he was. He knew that if he crossed the pen and went into the trees, always keeping the nest-barn at the same shoulder, and jumped through the trees until he reached the edge of those woods, he'd arrive at the drive. He knew that when he reached the drive, he would see the two long rows of maples. He knew that if he leaped across the drive and then from maple to maple up along it, back toward the nest-house, he would come to the wide-limbed horse chestnut tree. Toaff stared off into the woods, as if he could actually see those maples, and the drive, and that horse chestnut. He whuffled to himself, wondering if he was going to end up right back at the safe place where he had started out. Maybe he was a Lucky One after all.

That thought drove the whuffling out of him because it made him remember the limp gray body. In turn, this sad memory was driven off when Leaf cried out, "Toaff? Where are you?"

Toaff wheeled around. But he couldn't see her. Also, he couldn't see Neef or Tief, even if he could hear their voices, high and clear above the faint far-off hum of the chain saw.

"Toaff? Here we are!"

"Wait'll you see!"

The voices came from the little nest-house. Toaff scurried around a pole and into the grassy pen, and then he could see Tief and Neef inside the nest-house, their noses snuffling on the dirt floor. Leaf was climbing up into a top corner, where some boards joined up, like branches joined at the trunk of a tree.

The whole wide front of that nest-house was an entrance. Toaff ran over to explore it with the others. When he entered, Leaf called down to him, "We can build a drey up here, can't we, Toaff? We can build a big, deep drey up here, and it will be dry, and safe, too, with that top over our heads. No raptor could get through that top. Do you know how to build a drey?"

That, Toaff needed to think about, and he was having trouble thinking because the oily unpleasant smell was so strong in this nest-house, and there was something else, too, a tiny trail of bad smell. . . .

"Toaff!" Leaf insisted. "You *do* know how to build a drey. I know you do, you came outside long before we did, you've seen everything on the farm. Let's get to work." She whuffled sharply and happily and announced to them all, "This place is why the sheep wanted the dogs to tell us to come here. This is where we're supposed to live."

Toaff raised his nose to follow that thin trail as it wound in and out of the stronger smell. In its own way it was just as unpleasant as the oily one, but it was not as nasty as he happened to know it could be.

# INTRODUCING THE MICE

Toaff had recognized the smell of mouse. Where was the mouse?

Leaf was asking, "We could put a drey up here, couldn't we, Toaff? If we built one?"

Was the smell fading away? He couldn't be sure.

"Is a drey safe?" Neef worried.

Toaff turned his attention back to the Littles, and told them, "To build a drey, you need some branches thin enough to bend. Then you rest them close together on strong branches. Then you put leaves and dry grass all around and through them. That makes the bottom and the sides. Then you want new, soft grass, or even moss, to line the inside. There should be moss in the woods behind the stone wall, and there's dry grass right here."

"*I* can find branches!" Tief cried. "*I* can find moss! I find things!"

Leaf was already scrambling down to the ground. "Let Toaff finish," she said.

Toaff moved toward a loose pile of dry grass gathered up in one corner. "This is perfect for the sides of a drey."

Was the thin smell growing stronger? Was it coming out of this dry grass? "Unless it's damp," he said.

Before he could stick his nose into the mound, a high voice squeaked out from it, "It's not wet."

"But you can't take it," added a second high voice, and a third completed the thought, "Because it's *our* nest."

At that claim, three gray mice emerged from the hay and stood in a row, shaking off the bits and pieces of grass that clung to their heads and backs. "You're squirrels," one said, and "Aren't you?" squeaked the next, and then the third explained, "Because of your tails."

At the first strange squeaking sound, Leaf and Neef and Tief had all fled up to the high boards. They sat up on their haunches, chuk-chukking wildly to drive the strangers off. Because they were the Littles and didn't know any better, Toaff had to calm them down before he could talk to the mice. He called up, "It's all right. They're mice. They can't hurt you."

"Yes I could," the first mouse objected.

"If I wanted to," the second added, and the third completed the thought, "But I don't want to."

They stood in a line right in front of him, little noses pointing up, black beady eyes shining with curiosity, long tails stiff and high and brave. They were plump and smooth-skinned, with little round legs and delicate bones in their paws. Their tails were long and hairless. They were much smaller than the Littles, no bigger than a squirrel's back leg, and their boldness made Toaff want to whuffle.

"You're right, I am a squirrel, and so are those others," he said, in the friendliest voice he had. "My name is Toaff."

"And I'm Tief!" came the cry from above, which was quickly shushed by Leaf, who murmured, "Let Toaff take care of it."

The mice ignored the interruption. They introduced themselves as proudly as if they were the size of cats, "Fiddle," "Faddle," "Fuddle," and explained, "We're on our way to find the lake," then, "Uncle Fredle told us about it," finishing, "But I think we got lost."

At the mention of the lake, Tief and Neef, followed by a worried Leaf, came back down to stand on the ground behind Toaff to ask their own questions. "Did the sheep tell you to find the lake? They told us to come here. They never told *us* where the lake is."

"Sheep can't tell you anything," said a mouse, and the next added, "They don't know anything." The third explained, "They just do what the dogs tell them."

"You've got it backward," Leaf told them.

"It's the dogs who made the sheep leave this pen last spring," Fiddle argued.

"They'll make them come back in the fall," added Faddle.

"They showed us how to get here," Fuddle said, "because the dogs take care of us. Especially Sadie."

"There isn't any dog called Say-Dee," the Littles said.

"*Woo-hah, woo-hah,* they don't know anything!" the mice said to one another, and "We do, too!" answered the Littles.

199

But Toaff had a question, not a quarrel. "How do you know all those things about dogs and sheep? When you're so small?"

The three mice were glad to explain everything to the squirrels. They were house mice in winter, then they moved outside in warm weather, with Uncle Fredle. He was the bravest and smartest of any of them and they wanted to be just like him. Except now he was old and they didn't want to be old. They explained that house mice learned as much as they could from everyone on the farm, except spiders, of course, or ants, and nobody had anything to learn from chickens, and sheep weren't much better, and they had never understood a word said by the cows. Even the dogs couldn't understand sheep and cows—

The Littles interrupted. "You've got it all wrong," they argued. "Don't you know? It's the sheep who tell the dogs what to tell us to do."

The mice disagreed, "No they don't."

Before they could quarrel about that, too, Toaff asked the mice, "Can you understand what humans say?"

It turned out that the big white nest-house had a lot of smaller nests inside it, and one of these was called the kitchen. The humans were in and out of the kitchen, all day long, so a kitchen mouse heard humans talking all the time to one another. "And singing, too," said Fiddle. "Singing songs."

"Because sometimes they get tired of just using talking," explained Faddle.

"It's just Missus that sings," Fuddle reminded his brothers. "Mister and Angus are too busy, and Sadie takes care of the baby. Because the dogs take care of everybody, even the baby," he announced to the squirrels.

"Is singing all silvery, and long?" Toaff asked. *Singing* was the right word for that kind of sound. But the Littles had a different concern.

"When will the sheep get here?" they asked, and had an explanation of their own. "The sheep want us to meet them here."

"The sheep will come when the dogs tell them to," said Fiddle.

"They'll come when the dogs want them to," said Faddle.

"Because the dogs tell the sheep what to do," Fuddle reminded the Littles.

"You've got it backward," Leaf said.

"No, no!" said the mice, all together.

"*You* don't understand," said Fiddle.

"If you stay until winter, you will," said Faddle.

"Because the dogs will bring the sheep back for the winter," Fuddle explained.

Toaff interrupted again. "Can you show me singing?"

"Missus gave us our names," Fiddle announced.

"She sang about us," Faddle agreed.

"Because we're always together, all three of us," Fuddle explained.

"Three blind mice!" they squeaked in unison, and squeaked it again. "Three blind mice! See how they run! See how they run!" Then all three mice began to run around in circles, making high squeaking *woo-hah* sounds, until they got dizzy and began to stumble, and Fuddle tripped and landed on his nose, all three of them *woo-hah*ing all the while.

Their noises didn't sound in the least like the silvery sound, but also they did, sort of, almost, in a way. The kind of winding, moonlit sound Missus made was hidden somewhere in the middle of the squeaky blind-mice noises. *Singing,* Toaff said to himself. He was sure he couldn't do it, singing, not even in a ruined way like these mice, but he was glad to know its name. When he said the word softly to himself, inside his own head, he could almost hear her voice, singing.

# TOAFF CHANGES HIS MIND, AGAIN

Once the Littles had arrived behind the nest-barn and found the sheep pen there, all they wanted to do was wait for the sheep to arrive, and wonder how long it would be, and talk about how glad the sheep would be to see that the squirrels had done as they were told. If Toaff suggested they practice moving through the woods, climbing up and down trunks and jumping from tree to tree, "We have to be *here*," the Littles argued.

"Why do we need to know how to jump?" Tief asked, and Leaf explained, "We don't need to jump, here behind the nest-barn." And when Toaff wanted to show them where pine and fir and spruce cones, and horse chestnuts and acorns, too, could be found, because it was time to gather stores for the long winter that was coming, Neef objected. "The sheep are going to take care of us. They *said*."

It didn't take more than a day or two for the Littles to build their drey up in a high corner next to the nest-barn wall. And it didn't take them long to decide that this was what the sheep had planned all along. *And* it didn't take long after that for them to start disagreeing with one another. "Of course not all of the squirrels could get here," Tief said. "There's just room enough for us."

Toaff wondered, "Did the sheep want them to die?"

"How can we know what sheep want? But if it's what happened . . . ," Leaf answered.

"I wish our mother hadn't died," Neef said.

"She didn't mind. Don't be such a baby."

"I'm not! And you wish our mother was here too, so don't say you don't."

"I'm not!"

Toaff wasn't surprised to hear the Littles arguing. The danger that had bound them together was now safely behind them. They were no longer so afraid. They no longer felt so helpless and weak. They no longer needed one another for comfort and safety. Of course they didn't get along as well as they used to. But the Littles could fit more quarreling into a day than any other squirrels Toaff had ever lived with.

Toaff soon figured out that he didn't belong with the Littles any more than he had with the Lucky Ones. So, on the morning of the third day, he went off alone into the woods to find himself a den. A scattering of twigs and grass in a hollowed-out hole in an old maple tree might have been some other squirrel's abandoned nest and made a good start for his own. Had Soaff maybe lived in that nest?

That would make it a good place, he thought, and that afternoon he announced his move.

"What will the sheep think?" Leaf asked.

"The sheep don't know anything about me," Toaff pointed out.

"When we were lost, Say called you," Neef argued, "and the sheep tell the dogs what to do, so they must have told her to do that."

From under the little pile of hay on the ground came the voice of Fiddle, to remind them, "The dogs are in charge," and Faddle agreed, "The *dogs* told you to call him, because sheep can't even talk," while Fuddle had positive proof. "We know it," he said.

This diverted Leaf's attention ("No you don't!") and Tief disagreed, too ("Say told us his name"), while Neef just complained ("Those mice shouldn't say that about the sheep").

Toaff went off to work on the nest in his new den.

The nights grew colder, and their darkness lasted longer. During the days, the sun warmed everything up, unless there was no sun because it was cloudy, or raining. On not-rainy days, Toaff foraged. He had been right to think there would be good foraging in the woods. Pinecones were scattered all around and occasionally he came across some squirrel's forgotten hoard of buried acorns or horse chestnuts. He shared the food he found with the Littles and with the mice, too. He hadn't yet decided if he wanted to stay in these woods for the winter and see sheep, or if he wanted to go on to the horse chestnut tree, to get away from the quarreling.

It seemed that even when the squirrels were sharing both territory and food with the mice, the quarreling didn't stop. Sometimes it made Toaff whuffle, to see six little mouths all moving at once, each trio trying to tell the other it was wrong, twelve cross and impatient round black or beady black eyes glaring. Sometimes it just made him cranky. However, since he hadn't ever seen a sheep, he was curious. "Do they have fur?" he asked.

"It's thick, and it's soft. The softest part of our nest is that fur."

"I bet your new nest in the woods doesn't have anything that soft in it."

"Do they have tails?" Toaff asked. But this turned out to be the wrong question.

"Little fat wiggle-waggle tails. *Woo-hah.*"

"They wiggle-waggle their tails and go *bau-bau-bau.*"

"Silly sheep. *Woo-hah.*"

"Clumsy loud dogs," whuffled the Littles. "Yarking at everything."

Toaff wondered about all of it: the sheep he'd never seen and the dogs he could sometimes understand. He wondered which—if either—took care of squirrels, or if it was humans, or even crows, in charge. He wondered if he wanted to stay in the woods behind the nest-barn, all winter long. He knew that it might well be as good a place to live as a squirrel would ever find, but that didn't make him want to keep on living there. There was too much quarreling behind the nest-barn and now another argument had broken out in just the brief time he had sat back to wonder.

"Not true! It's sheep that aren't!"

"Not true! It's dogs!"

"Sheep are bigger!"

"Dogs are faster! And smarter!"

"Not true, not true!"

Toaff interrupted. "Can't we please talk about something else?"

A silence answered his question. Then all six of them turned on him. "No!"

Maybe being told no like that by all of them together made up Toaff's mind as much as all the quarreling. But before he left, he tried one last time to help the Littles. "You need more than just a warm nest for winter. You also need lots of stores."

"The sheep will feed us," Leaf promised him from the edge of the drey.

"Not if the dogs don't want them to," Fiddle called up from the pile of dry grass.

"Dogs aren't the boss!"

"Yes they are!"

Right then was when Toaff left them behind. He didn't say goodbye to the mice or to the Littles, and none of them asked where he was going. They were too busy quarreling.

# AN UNKNOWN ENEMY!
# AN UNEXPECTED ALLY!

Day was ending as Toaff slipped through the thick woods, running, climbing, and jumping, moving quickly from spruce to birch to pine, making his way back to his old territory. He was thinking about how it felt to join the crows in their sky, even if for a brief time, to be flying, almost, and he was looking forward to the long leap over the drive, and he was hoping he would find a good place for a den in the horse chestnut tree. Thinking and remembering and hoping made Toaff move fast. He scrambled down trunks and dashed along the ground to the next pine, then climbed up it to make the short jump across to a slim young beech. He raced along through the gathering dusk, happily but—and this was his mistake—not warily.

His ears warned him first. He heard . . . heard something . . . maybe . . . but what? He stopped on the ground under a low pine branch and listened.

Faint machine noises hummed in the distance, and a dog yarked sharply somewhere beyond the nest-barn. But those sounds had been in the air all afternoon. It wasn't those sounds that made the skin on his neck want to crawl up to hide in his ears.

Toaff stayed still as stone.

Birds chirped to one another and the tiny voices of insects hummed steadily, and beneath that layer of noise lay the deep silence of the woods on a windless fall evening. But in that deep silence there was something quiet going on, something that troubled him. Something almost silent. Something so noiseless it made Toaff uneasy. His ears strained to hear that whatever-it-was. He huddled back against a thick pine root and tried to see into the shadows.

Nothing moved. Even the needles on the thinnest pine branches were motionless. Toaff's tail was up, and his eyes searched among the trunks and bushes, and nothing moved.

But he sensed *something*.

Toaff peered into the tangle of bushes and branches. He listened into the empty spaces between familiar sounds. He sniffed at the crisp, earthy air.

He smelled nothing and heard nothing and saw nothing.

Until a sudden, rough *kaah-kaah* alerted him and he saw it—no more than a quivering of shadows. *Kaah-kaah* slashed through the air again—a warning? *What is—?*

He bolted. He scrambled up into the pine, and when he came to a high branch he turned to look. When Toaff looked, he saw that he *couldn't* have identified the thing. It was nothing he had ever seen before. It was the size of a cat, but not a cat, and it was silent and quick as a cat,

211

but a cat able to climb up tree trunks and go down them squirrel-fashion, headfirst. This thing was more dangerous even than a cat.

Toaff jumped and scrambled and ran. He fled through the trees, sometimes on the ground, sometimes leading the not-cat up a trunk, then circling so quickly down that the not-cat was surprised, sometimes shifting directions suddenly, and sometimes he'd gain a little ground that way. But the not-cat was faster than a squirrel. It kept catching up, coming closer. Maybe this thing couldn't leap like a squirrel? That was his only hope and Toaff raced for the drive, where a squirrel could leap out and across between maples and be safe. Maybe.

Toaff fled. The not-cat came after him. He turned once again, just to see it. It had sharp, curved teeth. It had a little pointed face and hungry eyes. When he saw those eyes, Toaff ran even faster, even more desperately, to escape.

Trees appeared in front of him, and some he scrambled up and some he circled, but the not-cat was catching up. It was so close behind him that if Toaff had tried to climb, it would have been close enough to sink its teeth into Toaff's rump, so he switched direction again, to go along the ground. He had to dash out onto dirt, and across the dirt. The not-cat came after him—fast—and Toaff was past the maples and in the pasture grass before he knew it. So he ran through long grass toward where his old dead pine had stood in that long-ago winter, when he had been safe in a nest in a safe den with a lot of other squirrels. The pasture offered no shelter, no place to hide, so he had to keep running. He could hear the not-cat breathing behind him—getting too close, and he knew it—

He tried to go even faster, but the breathing came even closer, and it was loud as wind—

Without any thought, without even the beginning of an idea, Toaff wheeled around—because the windy breath wasn't the not-cat after all and he had realized it too late. The windy breath was the sweep of wings. It was a raptor. He knew this, and knew he was finished, even as he stumbled back toward the drive, running right into the teeth of the not-cat. The not-cat tore at his face.

Toaff's legs kept moving.

The not-cat was on top of him.

Then it was gone and Toaff kept going, stumbling across the drive to curl up under a bush and die. He was too weak and shocked to climb. He was trembling too hard to be able to burrow, or even look for a root to huddle behind.

Maybe the crows *had* tried to save him—or maybe not—but that didn't matter because their warning cries hadn't come in time. He didn't understand exactly what was wrong with him, but he knew that something had happened to his face. He knew this not just by the blood seeping down into his mouth but also by the pain. Then he closed the one eye he could still open, and dropped into the dark.

# NILF TO THE RESCUE

When Toaff came to himself, he wasn't dead and his face hurt and he could hear low, soft voices. He didn't move.

He didn't want to move, for fear the pain would get worse, and he didn't dare to move until he understood where he was. He didn't even open his eyes. In fact, he wasn't sure that he *could* open one of them, on the side of his face a raptor's talon had ripped at. Unless it was the side of his face a hunter's fangs had ripped at. That made no difference to Toaff. He lay motionless, and listened. Trying to figure out why the soft, chur-churring voices were familiar. Trying to stay awake.

"Dead, I'm sure of it."

"If you're so sure then *you* go see."

"Where'd he come from? Where are the rest of them?"

"I don't see any more. Do you? Do you think it's a trap? Let's get out of here."

"That holly bush might be protecting him. It can't be, but is it?"

"Hollies don't take care of Grays. Just us."

"But he's under its branches."

"But why is he here? Do you think they're planning an attack?"

"I wouldn't worry. Some fox or maybe the fisher will smell this greedy Gray and if he isn't dead now he will be by morning."

They whuffled.

Toaff couldn't move and he couldn't think. He fell asleep right where he was, on the dirt ground with no more than the spindly branches of a holly bush for cover.

It was hunger that woke him. Hunger and a crow, calling.

Calling *him*? Toaff didn't know. The crow could have been telling another crow where food was. Or the *kaah-kaah* could have been a warning. How could Toaff know? He just knew that the cry had woken him up and reminded him that he wasn't safe on the ground, where any hunting animal could smell him and find him. Toaff would make an easy prey.

He sat up. Both eyes could open and he could see clearly.

He saw that he was in the woods, although not very far from the drive, and he saw a low-branched spruce close by. Before he had even made up his mind to do it, he began to move.

His movements were slow, clumsy. Moving *hurt*. First safety and then food, he told himself. You're alive, he reminded himself, and at that moment he heard a soft voice from behind the low bush where he'd been lying.

"Toaff?"

Toaff stopped.

"Is that you?"

Toaff turned around.

"It *is* you. I thought so."

"Nilf? What are you doing here?"

The little red squirrel whuffled as he came up beside Toaff. "It's where I live. Don't you remember?" He was plumper than he had been and looked stronger, although, being a Churrchurr, he would never be as plump and strong as Toaff.

"Let's get you up into this spruce," Nilf said.

What was Nilf doing, being the one to decide what should be done? Toaff felt a little flash of crossness. "What do you think I was doing? Before you interrupted." He forced himself to move as fast as he could, which wasn't nearly as fast as he would have liked, and Nilf stayed at his side, chattering.

Toaff remembered, now, how the little squirrel had chattered.

"Once you're safe, I'll find you a pinecone. I think you must be hungry. But this is our territory. Did you forget about that? Why are you here? What happened to you? Did you forget me? No, because you know my name. Aren't you going to say anything, Toaff?"

Toaff couldn't move and talk at the same time. He kept moving.

When they got to the rough trunk of the spruce, Nilf

halted. He asked, "*Did* you sneak up from the other end of the woods to find out about us so you Grays can drive us out? I don't think you did, but you didn't, did you?"

Toaff didn't answer. He didn't stop moving. It took all of his concentration and strength to climb as far as the lowest of the branches. But he did it. There, he crouched close to the trunk and waited to feel better.

"You didn't eat any of the holly berries, did you?" Nilf asked suddenly, from the ground right below him.

"No," Toaff said. "I don't think I ate anything. There was—I think it was a hawk, and before that there was—"

"Because if you did, I shouldn't even try to help you," Nilf said. "Because . . . Don't you know that the holly bushes don't want their berries to get eaten?"

What did this have to do with holly bushes? Toaff wondered, but Nilf had gone off. He returned with a pinecone for Toaff, saying, "Move along, give me room," then asking, "What got you?"

"I don't know," Toaff said. "It was almost a cat, but it was a better climber, and furrier."

"The fisher," Nilf told him. "He's worse than a fox. Much worse. You're lucky you got away. How did you get away?"

Toaff was trying to remember more clearly. "I didn't see the hawk, if it was a hawk. It could have been an eagle, maybe. I didn't really see anything. I was running and I twisted away when it dove for me and it missed me and when it came back it got the other thing. The fisher? Instead of me."

217

"Well," Nilf said, taking a good look at the side of Toaff's head. "Something didn't *exactly* miss you."

"I'll be fine," Toaff said, and he knew that was true.

"There's something wrong with your face," Nilf pointed out, and unexpectedly he began to whuffle. "You look—" but he couldn't finish what he was going to say, because of whuffling.

Crossness flashed inside of Toaff again, but then he began to whuffle, too, because he had escaped the fisher, which was a more dangerous hunter than even a fox, and the hawk or maybe eagle had missed him, and whatever Mroof and Pneef might think, he *was* lucky. He was alive, and eating seeds from the pinecone Nilf had found, feeling his stomach fill up. Gladness bubbled up in him. He couldn't help but whuffle, too, waiting for Nilf to tell him, "What *do* I look like?"

"Like"—*whuffle, whuffle*—"like . . ." Nilf couldn't seem to stop whuffling and neither could Toaff.

# NILF EXPLAINS EVERYTHING

Toaff never heard whatever it was Nilf thought he looked like because right then a throng of red squirrels surged around the trunk of the spruce and a few even scurried up it, to hover above the branch where Toaff and Nilf were sitting. The air filled with their voices: "Get out!" "Out of the way, Nilf!" "We'll bite!" "Ours!"

Toaff tensed. He could jump, he reminded himself. He could outjump these Churrchurrs.

"Hey!" Nilf chittered. Actually, he squealed it, in a high, frightened voice. He had to repeat himself several times before he got their attention. "Hey! Stop! Wait!"

"*Now* what, Nilf?" one of the red squirrels demanded. "What's your problem *now*?"

"This is the one," Nilf churred. "I told you about him. He saved me."

"He's a Gray," another red squirrel pointed out. "In case you haven't noticed."

"He saved me," Nilf insisted.

"He's a spy who came to find out about us."

"No I'm not!" Toaff cried, even though he didn't expect them to believe him. Squirrels prefer to believe what they have already made up their minds about.

"He saved me," Nilf repeated. "When you just left me there."

"You fell and you didn't move. You were trying one of your crazy stunts."

"You left me for foxfood."

"What were we supposed to do? We thought you were dead."

"But I wasn't, was I?" Nilf pointed out. "*And*," he added in the silence that greeted that fact, "Toaff taught me how to jump."

More silence. Then, "You know his name?" a voice asked.

"I *told* you. He took me to his den, and he fed me too. So I want to let him go."

"We can't do that, Nilf."

"Didn't we find him under a holly bush?" Nilf asked, which made no sense at all to Toaff. "Think about it," Nilf insisted. "Why do you think we found him under a holly bush?"

*Because that's where I was,* Toaff didn't say out loud. He'd forgotten how irritating Nilf could be.

But the Churrchurrs seemed to be taking Nilf seriously. They chur-churred nervously among themselves. Finally one came forward. He stood on the ground right below the branch where Nilf was sitting, with Toaff just beyond him. "All right," the Churrchurr said. "He can go. But you have to make sure he goes all the way. And he can never come back. Understood?" He looked right at Toaff. "Do you understand?"

"Yes," said a greatly relieved Toaff, who, it turned out, was not all that confident of his ability to outjump and outrun so many Churrchurrs in his weakened state.

"Understood," said Nilf, and when he glanced at Toaff, his dark eyes within their white circles sparkled wildly with the victory.

They weren't very far from the drive. When they had climbed up a maple, the first thing Toaff looked for was a horse chestnut tree. It stood where he remembered, spreading out wide branches from which half of the leaves had already fallen and those that were left drooped down, brown. He saw the big white nest-house and then, looking the other way, the lines of maples with the drive curving between them. At the end of the pasture, across the drive, were the woods beyond, just as he remembered. Everything he saw was familiar.

Nilf was looking back behind them while Toaff was looking ahead, and Toaff finally asked, "What about the holly bushes makes you think they . . . ," but he didn't know how to finish his question without sounding as if he was starting a quarrel. He thought for a minute, then asked the same question, but differently.

"Are the holly bushes something special the Churr-churrs keep for food?"

"No!" cried Nilf. "We never would! They take care of us. We'd *never* eat them, no matter how hungry we were." He explained, "Where there's a holly bush, it's a good place for us. Away from Grays. Near food and safe for burrows. The holly bushes take care of us."

Toaff thought about that for a minute, then asked, "*All* squirrels? Or just all Churrchurrs?"

"Not everybody agrees," Nilf said, and he added, "But I think all of all of us, every squirrel there is." Then he changed the subject quickly, as if he didn't want to talk about it anymore. "Where will you go?"

But Toaff told him, "I'd think it would *have* to be every squirrel, but how do you know it's what hollies do?"

"I don't, not really. I wonder, sometimes. But I think maybe," Nilf said.

They looked at one another for a time that didn't feel long, although it might have been. Then Nilf asked again, "Where will you go now?"

As soon as he had seen the row of tall maples and the familiar pasture, Toaff had decided. "To where I used to live. I'll find a den or I'll make a drey."

"Aren't you going to join the other Grays?"

"What other Grays? I never saw any on my side of the drive. Besides, even if there are some, why would I want to join up with them?"

"Because . . . because Grays always gather as many as

you can all together when you're getting ready to drive us out of our territory."

"I don't want to drive you out of your territory," Toaff said, and he meant it. Although, even as he said it, and meant it, he had to remember the talk in his den that long-ago winter afternoon. He remembered how Old Criff hated the little red squirrels, and didn't trust them, and how everyone—except him—had seemed to agree with Old Criff. "I *don't*," he repeated.

"Well, some Grays have moved into *our* woods," Nilf reported. "They're so wild, and fierce, they don't even mind being close to the road. You know about the road, don't you?"

"I've never seen it," Toaff admitted.

"Neither have I, but I know it's more dangerous even than the fisher, or an eagle. There are no holly bushes anywhere near the road, but those Grays aren't afraid of anything. Everyone knows it's just a matter of time before they attack. To drive us out. They hate us and we hate them."

Toaff protested. "You don't hate *me*, do you?"

"The rest of us do," Nilf answered. Reminding himself of that seemed to change something. He raised his tail high and announced, "We're evened up now. You saved me and I saved you and now I'm going back to where I belong."

"I'm glad you were there," Toaff said. "Thank you. I don't hate you," he added.

"Neither do I," Nilf admitted.

"And I don't plan to start," Toaff said.

"Neither do I, but you can't come back," Nilf warned.

"I'm not saying goodbye," Toaff warned him right back.

Nilf whuffled. "Neither am I," he agreed.

# A NEW DEN IN AN OLD PLACE

Toaff didn't watch Nilf go away. He was busy going away himself, and besides, he knew they would meet up again, sometime. He had saved the Churrchurr's life and the Churrchurr had saved his life, and now they belonged to-gether, whatever any other Grays or Churrchurrs had to say about it. But Toaff had a den to find and a nest to build. He leaped across the drive, landing on a long maple branch that stretched toward him from the pasture side. He ran along that branch until he came to the rough, solid trunk, where he rested, waiting to be ready to go on. In that stop-rest-go-on manner, he traveled all the way up the drive to the horse chestnut tree.

He hoped there might be a den waiting there, or a drey. He didn't really think there would be but he hoped any-way. When a crow *kaah-kaah*ed in the pasture beside him, Toaff knew that *kaah-kaah* could mean anything. What a *kaah-kaah* really meant, he decided, was *Be alert!* Which was always good advice for a squirrel.

He got to the horse chestnut, climbed up, and sat look-ing around. In one direction he saw the low stone wall by the apple trees and the grass around the nest-house, flat and brown after the cold fall nights. In the other direction he saw the two firs standing guard next to a flat circle that was all that was left of his dead pine, and the pasture, and the woods beyond. Most important, just below where he sat on the horse chestnut trunk he saw a ragged, shallow dent where a branch had been ripped off. A den there would be high enough to be safe from ground-bound hunters like foxes and low enough within the tree's branches to keep a squirrel safe from raptors.

And from the fisher, too?

At the memory, Toaff shivered. He tried not to remember. He reminded himself that he'd never seen the fisher before, and he'd never heard of it either, so maybe it didn't like to hunt so close to where humans lived. Probably its territory was in the woods on the other side of the drive. Probably it was dead, anyway, and he didn't have to worry about it. If he ever saw a fisher in this pasture, *that* was the time to worry. Now wasn't the time for anything but finding a place to nest until he had made himself a den for the winter.

In not very long he'd found an empty bird's nest, comfortable enough for temporary shelter, and scrambled down to forage around the horse chestnut. A squirrel with a den in this tree could spend the long winter in comfort, Toaff knew. All around its roots lay chestnuts, kept safe within their spiny shells. Nearby, the branches of the two fir trees were filled with cones. Not too far away, the slim trunks of the apple trees were surrounded by fruit. This had always been a good place, Toaff knew. That night, as darkness filled the air, Toaff curled up in a bird's nest high in the horse chestnut tree, with his tail wrapped around him, a full stomach, and a plan.

Day after day, Toaff used his teeth to hollow out a den, gnawing deep into the horse chestnut. The days were already much shorter and the nights longer and colder, and he knew it wasn't long before winter would bring snow, and cold winds. He wanted his den to lie deep within the broad trunk of the tree, protected from harsh winter weather. Day after day, Toaff chewed and clawed at the wood, and while he worked, the last long chestnut leaves drifted down from their branches.

When the hollow space was large enough, Toaff gathered twigs and dried grass. He added two black crow feathers to the sides and remembered the thick, soft sheep fur that the Littles had found. He was sorry he didn't have any of that to line his nest with. But the finished nest was comfortable enough, and he knew that the more nights he slept in it, the softer it would become.

Once he had a large den and a wide nest ready, Toaff set to work gathering stores. He buried mounds of the horse chestnuts in middens hidden among the roots of his tree. He carried pinecones and any seeds he found up into his den. He worked constantly, day after day, gathering. He didn't have to be told that winter would be long, and cold, and difficult to live through.

Every day, Toaff heard the dogs yarking and the humans talking, although not singing. Every day, machines traveled up and down the drive and Mister moved the cows into and out of the pasture to forage. Crows *kaah-kaah*ed. The cats stalked along beside the nest-house and slept in the sunny space in front of the nest-barn. Every day, Toaff wasn't alone on the farm—but he hadn't seen another gray squirrel for such a long time that he sometimes worried that he never again would.

# TOAFF TAKES A LOOK AROUND

As worries often do, this worry led Toaff directly to an idea: *What if I take a look around?*

He had the idea and then he waited for several days to see if he kept on thinking it was a good one. He knew how much his legs liked leaping and how much his curiosity wanted to find out about the Grays Nilf had talked about; he also knew that a bad idea could lead to trouble. So he waited, to be as sure as he could be.

When he decided that he was sure enough, he set off. That late-fall morning, the air was cold, the wind was sharp, and clouds covered the whole sky. Toaff took a deep happy breath and leaped along down the drive, away from the nest-house, to take a look around.

The drive turned out to be longer than he had expected but Toaff didn't mind that, not at all. He had regained his full strength, and a longer drive meant more leaping, from one maple to another to another, and another after that. He kept to his side of the drive, first moving beside the pasture and then leaping along from tree to tree by the woods beyond. There, at every maple, he stopped to listen, and look, and sniff the air, but there were no signs of gray squirrels. He heard no chuk-chukking in the trees and saw no scurrying movement on the trunks. Once, perched high in a maple, he called out, "Anyone? Anyone here?" and there was no answer. It seemed that no squirrel had discovered the woods beyond and of course Toaff wondered what it would be like to live in a place where you were the first squirrel ever to be there, and to forage for stores where no other squirrel had ever put down a paw. Everything would be new. Nothing would be known. It would be frightening and exciting, and maybe wonderful.

He wondered if he would be more only, or less, if he was the first.

Wondering, Toaff leaped through patches of shadows and splotches of sunlight until, looking ahead to where the next maple should have been, he saw the way forward blocked by a wide black strip. The strip looked hard, and unpleasant. It reminded him of the drive, but it was much darker and wider and straighter. Toaff sat in the last maple, looking down at it. He looked, and listened, and sniffed. The air tasted unpleasant, like machines, and that led him to guess that the strip was probably the road. It certainly looked the way a dangerous thing should, dark and unwelcoming. More woods grew on the other side, and hadn't Braff said that was where he was going? Toaff wondered if he dared to try to cross the road.

At that moment something roared, and charged straight toward him. A huge, loud thing swept up the probably-a-road, right beneath the branch Toaff sat on. The wind that raced with it pulled at the branch with so much power, he was almost sucked off.

Toaff dug his nails in and held on.

The huge thing roared under him and thundered off along the probably-a-road. Trembling, Toaff scurried back to the safety of the trunk. He waited until the last echoes had died away and the tree branches had stopped waving. He couldn't even guess what he had seen. It looked like a machine, but bigger, higher, louder, and longer, and no machine he'd ever seen went that fast. He had barely had time to see it but he was pretty sure it *was* some kind of machine, with round legs to run on and no paws. If he had been in the middle of the road, he'd have been squashed flat. There was no way a squirrel could outrun that machine. If a squirrel was on the road and one of those things came along, then goodbye, squirrel.

This taking a look around was at an end.

He turned to go back along the drive. He wanted to get far from the road, and fast. But after a long leap from the second to the third maple, he heard an unfamiliar voice. He halted.

A voice?

"Toaff!"

The voice came out of the woods across the drive and

seemed to have no body attached to it. It was as if a tree knew his name, and called to him.

That trees couldn't talk, he was sure of. Wasn't he?

"I know you're Toaff," the tree said.

This was as bad as the road, except entirely different. *What should I—?*

A large gray squirrel jumped out into view on a branch of the maple just across the drive. "You *are* Toaff," he announced.

Toaff recognized him. "Braff," he said.

"It took you long enough to find us," Braff said, and he turned away. "Let's go," he said over his shoulder, and when Toaff didn't move, he asked, "*Now* what are you waiting for?"

Toaff felt shoved back into the nest in the dead pine, where he didn't know anything and Braff knew everything. This was not a good feeling. He remembered the last quarrel he'd had with Braff. "I thought you were going across the road," he said, and stayed right where he was.

"The crows warned us not to," Braff answered. "We were going to. We weren't afraid and we got to the road. We came right to the edge of it. It's easy to know you're at the edge because—"

"I've been there."

"Humph," said Braff. "Maybe you have. Maybe you haven't. But we were about to run across when the crows showed us what happens when an animal goes on the road.

They showed us. . . . It was something dead, something with long thin legs, right in front of us, all broken and bloody and out on the road. . . . The road got it."

Now Braff's voice got so low Toaff could barely hear what he was saying.

"The crows were carrying it away, but it was too big for them to take all at once and it looked almost as if they were eating it. . . ." Braff stopped speaking, to swallow twice. "It wasn't nice to see but they knew we needed to. They wanted to warn us not to touch the road."

"Oh," said Toaff, who wasn't sure any squirrel could figure out what a crow meant, and also suspected that it was a machine, not the road, that did the damage, but knew better than to try to tell Braff anything.

"Anyway, Soaff will be glad to see you," Braff said.

"Soaff?" Toaff asked. He thought of his other litter-mate. Soaff was a soft, safe memory, as welcome as summer mornings. "Where is she? How will I find her?"

"You just did. Follow me."

"I have my own nest now," Toaff answered. "In the horse chestnut tree."

Braff was silent. "Humph," he said eventually. "Well then," he said. "If that's the way you want to be," he said. "But when you decide to come over, remember to tell the guard to come get me."

"A guard? You have guards? Why?"

"What's *wrong* with you, Toaff? We have to have guards so the Churrchurrs don't sneak in and steal from the middens we've been filling. They live in part of this woods, closer to the nest-barn, in case you've forgotten. Winter's coming, in case you haven't noticed. We need guards so when the Churrchurrs attack, we won't be taken by surprise."

"Why would Churrchurrs attack you?"

"To drive us away. So they can steal our stores."

Toaff couldn't think how to show Braff that this wasn't true. He couldn't think what to do, but just then three crows came *kaah-kaah*ing into the sky behind him, flying low, close to the tops of the pines. What if they were telling him something about those woods?

"You could move across the drive into *these* woods," he told Braff. "You could carry your stores across, and over here you wouldn't have to worry about Churrchurrs."

"I'm not running away from any Churrchurr."

"No other squirrels live in these woods."

"They'd think we're afraid of them and get greedier. They hate us."

"But Braff, they say *you're* going to attack *them*, to steal *their* supplies, and take over *their* territory," Toaff explained.

"That just goes to show," Braff answered. "They're liars as well as thieves."

"But *all* squirrels steal from other squirrels," Toaff pointed out.

"Not like *they* do," Braff maintained. "You don't know anything, Toaff. But I've got to get back to my post. I'm on guard. It's important work. If any one of those Churrchurrs shows even his nose, he'll be sorry. I can promise you that," and Braff was gone.

Toaff went back up the drive, slowly and a little sadly, thinking. He knew what he knew about Churrchurrs and he thought what he thought about crows. But he was the only squirrel who wondered about things. Except maybe Nilf, was his first thought, and I wonder if Soaff does, the next, after which he felt a lot better.

# FIRST SADIE, THEN ANGUS, THEN THE HUMANS

On a cloudy morning that was cold as ice, Toaff ran up into a maple. The air smelled of something he half remembered, but he had another idea for the morning and didn't follow that memory to wherever it might lead. He leaped from maple to maple along the drive, from the first to the second tree, from the second to the third, and from there to the fourth, which had two long strong branches stretching across to the woods across the drive. Where Nilf lived.

Toaff sat there for a long time, hoping the little red squirrel would come. In all the time he waited, however, he didn't hear any chur-churring and he began to wonder, worrying—or began to worry, wondering—Had the Churrchurrs been driven away by Braff's Grays? But he didn't see or hear any gray squirrels either. He hoped that nothing had happened to change everything, because he had the idea that if he and Nilf could get along, so could other Grays and Churrchurrs. When he was with Nilf, eating together and talking, Toaff knew for sure and certain that this was true. He didn't want to forget Nilf and he didn't want Nilf to forget him. Someday, he was sure of it, he would arrive at the maple and see Nilf, waiting for him across the drive.

On his way back Toaff found a fat pinecone and carried it over to the stone wall, where he sat to dig out seeds, and eat them, and feel sad not to have found Nilf waiting, and watch anything that might happen.

"Hello! Hello!" a dog yarked. It was Sadie, and she was running right at him.

Toaff dropped the pinecone and squeezed between two of the stones.

Sadie crouched down to stick her nose in at him. Her nose was black, and wet, and he squeezed back even farther.

"Squirrel?" she asked.

"It's me, Toaff." Maybe she could remember him from the summer. Maybe she would recognize his smell and not come digging after him. If she started digging, maybe a bite on that wet black nose would get rid of her.

"What?" asked Sadie. "What? Play!" she yarked.

This was a word he knew, even when a dog yarked it so close to his ears that it was almost too loud to hear anything.

"Play!" Sadie yarked again. She jumped back away from the wall, and waited.

Toaff didn't move.

"Run! Chase! Play!" she insisted.

Toaff had to whuffle. He was pretty sure that dogs weren't supposed to ask squirrels to play.

But then, squirrels weren't supposed to understand it when dogs did. So, still whuffling, he kept backing up until he came out on the other side of the low wall and could scramble up to the top. "Can't catch me!" he chukked.

"What?" yarked Sadie. Her long furry tail waved. "Play?"

Toaff knew she wouldn't understand much of anything he said, so he just ran. He scurried along the top of the wall and Sadie ran after him, yarking, "Chase! Catch!" He scurried in and out through the stones, while Sadie chased after him, and couldn't catch him, and tried to jump on him, and missed. He dashed and dodged, always keeping ahead of her, making sure to never escape. She ran and twisted, jumped and yarked.

Then Angus bounded up. "Squirrel, Sadie? Where?"

Toaff fled up the chestnut trunk to a safe branch. Sadie waited below, looking up, her tail waving. "We play!" she told Angus.

"Squirrels don't play," Angus told Sadie.

"Play!" she yarked up at Toaff.

With Angus there, Toaff knew better than to move.

"You run! I chase!" Sadie reminded him, and jumped around in excitement.

Toaff didn't move.

"I told you," said Angus. "Silly Sadie. Don't *yark* anything. Come! Now!"

Sadie stared up at Toaff for a while before she followed Angus to wherever he had said she had to be, and Toaff was sorry to see her go.

But she came back that same day, in the afternoon. Just before she returned, for the first time since winter ended three seasons ago, snow started falling through the air, and Toaff realized what that smell in the air had been. Snow coming, of course. This was too delicate a snow to do more than put a light white cover over the clumps of brown grass and the top of the nest-house, but the air tasted of more snow, coming soon. Sadie bounded up to the wall, and began to stick her nose into the narrow spaces between the stones, yarking, "Play?"

"Here! Up here!" Toaff chukked. He ran down the horse chestnut and they began a wild run-and-chase game, up and down and around the wall and between the trees. Sadie ran—"Stop! Run!"—on the ground below while Toaff leaped from maple to maple. Sometimes he scrambled down the trunk, chukking, "Can't catch me! Can't catch me!" Until they both had to stop, to catch their breath and get ready for the next wild running-and-chasing.

That was when they heard the coughing sound. Both animals turned to look.

Missus stood in the drive with the baby beside her and they were both watching. *Gha-gha-gha*, Missus coughed, *gha-gha-gha*, and she called something to Sadie.

"Goodbye, squirrel!" Sadie yarked before she ran off to snuffle her nose into the baby's face.

Even though he knew she wouldn't understand him, Toaff called after her, "Goodbye, Sadie! Come back soon!"

That snow didn't last long. As soon as it stopped, Mister walked right up to the trunk of Toaff's tree, carrying something in one of his front paws. Toaff wanted to slip back into his warm shadowy den, and hide, but what if Mister was going to start cutting down branches to drive the squirrels away? Mister didn't have his orange head and what he carried didn't look like the chain saw, but Toaff was ready to get out fast, if he needed to. He crouched in his entrance. If he saw the chain saw, he wouldn't need to find out more, because once he saw the chain saw, he would know.

Mister didn't notice a squirrel nose barely sticking out in the cold air. All of his attention was on the thing he was carrying. He held it up against the trunk, and then Toaff could see that it was a feeder. Holding the feeder, Mister began to hit it—*thwap*—as if it was the garbage-nest, *thwappety-thwap*, hit, hit, hit. When he took his paw away, the feeder stayed up. But Mister didn't leave.

Was he waiting for the Lucky Ones? Toaff looked for them, coming up the stone wall from the apple trees or coming around the corner of the big white nest-house. But Mroof and Pneef didn't appear. Instead, Mister reached into his fur and pulled out something brown from under it, something he held up over the platform of the feeder, something with a *clickety-clickety* sound, something he took down again after a short time. After that, Mister just went away, and Toaff was none the wiser. He waited to learn more.

Eventually curiosity got the better of him and he climbed cautiously down the trunk to find out just what Mister had been up to.

He approached the feeder from above, slowly. It was not on a pole, like the one near the nest-house, and it wasn't hanging down from a branch, like the suet the Lucky Ones had told him the humans put out in winter. Maybe this wasn't a feeder at all. Maybe it was a trap.

The feeder had a top like a nest-house but its two ends were open, like entrances, so it couldn't be a trap, could it? The trunk made one long side of the feeder and the opposite side was hard and clear, like an entrance into the humans' nest-house. Toaff stood on the top, peering down and around over its edge. He could see right into it. Inside, flat gray seeds and little yellow seeds spread out all over the feeder's floor.

Would humans want to give a squirrel his own feeder?

Unlikely as it seemed, Toaff guessed maybe they must, since that was what they seemed to have done. He didn't understand humans at all. First they cut down branches if a squirrel came too close to their nest-house, then they put up a feeder and filled it with seeds as if they wanted squirrels to stay nearby.

Toaff didn't understand why humans would do that. It was a puzzle he hoped he'd have a seed-filled winter to think about. And if Grays couldn't understand Churrchurrs, and vice versa, and they were all squirrels, how could a squirrel expect to understand a human?

# WINTER
# AGAIN

# AN UNEXPECTED GUEST

Winter settled gently down, all over the farm. Days were short and cold. Nights were long and colder. Toaff's fur grew thicker, so that whether he foraged and piled up stores, or went down to the feeder for food, or played with Sadie, he was always warm. The humans, too, he noticed, had thicker fur in cold weather.

Every now and then a human put more seeds into his feeder, but no squirrel ever arrived to share them. The dogs were often outside, and whenever she could, Sadie joined him for a game of run-and-chase, but often she couldn't because Angus came after her, yarking about *jobs*. The crows flew black across the sky and came to rest on the bare branches of maple and horse chestnut trees. Sometimes they shared Toaff's feeder. Missus and the baby no longer visited the garden and Mister no longer came out with the lawn mower. Toaff heard soft *bau-bau*ing, sometimes, and *muuh-muuh*ing from the nest-barn morning and evening, and there was yarking and *kaah-kaah*ing, but no chuk-chukking and no chur-churring either, not that Toaff could hear, even when he went down to the fourth maple and found Nilf waiting. He told Nilf about the feeder.

"Don't you wonder why he did that?" Nilf asked, and "Maybe because it's winter," Toaff suggested, and "Could be," Nilf agreed. There was a lot of only in Nilf, Toaff decided, just like in Sadie, and could there be some in Missus, who had stared right at him? He wondered what Nilf would have to say about that idea and he was sorry not to be able to ask Sadie about it; but especially, he was glad to be exactly the squirrel he was.

Soon the fallen snow didn't melt away under the sunlight, because the sunlight was no longer warm. Toaff spent the long nights alone in his den, so he always chose to come outside during the day, even just to watch machines move up and down the drive. Then snow came down thickly, all one day and into the night, and turned the farm winter white.

After that first heavy snowfall, as the last light of a cold afternoon was being sucked from the sky by early-winter darkness, Toaff had filled his stomach at the feeder and was sitting on a low branch, waiting until it grew so dark he would have to go back into his den and sleep. The air was still, and silent, and in it a voice chukked his name.

"Toaff?"

The word rose up clear through the dim air. Toaff moved quietly around to the side of the tree that faced away from the nest-house. He looked out over the pasture.

"Toaff?"

It took him no time to run out along a branch and look down into the shadows and see Soaff's thick silver tail and round body. "Soaff!" he called down. "Up here! Come on up!" and in no time the two squirrels sat side by side on a bare branch just above the entrance to his den.

"Hello, Soaff." He was glad to see her, and then he said it again. "Hello, hello."

"I found you!" she told him.

"You did," he agreed. He didn't know how long she would stay, so he took a deep breath to begin. He wanted to tell her about everything. He wanted to tell her about the feeder, and playing with Sadie, and the danger of cats and escaping the fisher and the possibility of sometime, someday, once again hearing what the mice had called singing, which he couldn't describe with any words he knew. But she had things to tell him, too, and she started first.

"We moved across the drive. Into the woods at the end of the pasture. There are no other squirrels living there, just us. We all moved together and nobody got lost. Braff found it for us."

"That's good," he said, and wondered how long it would be before he could tell Nilf that the Churrchurrs didn't have to worry anymore. He remembered that he could tell Soaff about sheep and raccoons and the Lucky Ones.

"They have guards out, but nobody has seen any danger, but they want to keep the guards because they're afraid the Churrchurrs will track them down," Soaff told him. "I think they like being afraid but I don't."

"I don't blame you," he said, and now he remembered that he could tell her about Mister, when he wore his orange head and carried his chain saw, about how Mister had cut their dead pine into pieces and Toaff went to live in the apple trees.

Soaff said, "Because *you* don't hate them. The Churrchurrs, I mean. You don't, do you? I could tell, last winter, that you didn't. You're not afraid, like Braff and everyone, so I wanted to come live in your den."

"Oh," said Toaff. "You want to live in my den? Live with me?" He pictured his pile of stores and the seeds in his feeder. He pictured his nest, which was big enough for two squirrels. Then he thought about how long winter was and how fierce the winter storms could be and how much shorter the long nights would be if there was another squirrel to share them. He remembered how, when he had told Soaff about leaping, she had wanted to do it, too, and about how comfortable it was to curl up in a nest beside her, and about how she didn't like to argue. Maybe there was some only in her, too. For sure, they belonged together. "That's a very good idea, Soaff," he said.

In fact, it was such a good idea that he felt like running out to the end of the branch, and leaping, leaping out and across, and then leaping back again. He had all winter to tell Soaff about Nilf, and the Churrchurrs, and everything else that he had seen. All the long, cold, snowy season, they could tell stories, the old stories and the stories that had happened to them, in spring and summer and fall. Maybe in winter they could go see the sheep behind the nest-barn. Maybe in spring they would visit the apple trees together. Toaff hadn't been lonely living alone, because squirrels don't get lonely, but he was glad of this company, because squirrels like company.

# CAN A TREE GROW LIGHTS?

Late the next afternoon Mister and both dogs came out of the nest-barn together, just after the sun had dropped out of sight, leaving the air full of a fading light. Toaff sat on a branch near his entrance and kept an eye on them. Mister headed across the drive toward the horse chestnut tree.

Toaff didn't move.

In the still air, the *muuh-muuh*ing of cows was echoed by a soft *bau-bau*ing from behind the nest-barn. The crows were flying back to their nests, wherever they were, finished with the work of their day, whatever that was. They greeted one another quietly, *kaah-kaah, hello, hello.* Soaff had already gone inside, into the new, wider nest they had made, with the two black feathers still woven into its side. Mister and the dogs were usually inside at this darkening time of day. What were they doing outside?

Something white was curled around Mister's neck and hung down over his front legs, but he didn't seem worried by it, and neither did the dogs. Toaff didn't worry either; at least, not yet. He perched on a bare horse chestnut branch and waited to see what the human was doing this time. If there was danger, he'd call to Soaff and they'd make a run for it.

But Mister and the dogs went right by the horse chestnut tree and across the stone wall. They went right through the snow to where the two fir trees stood guard over the stump of the dead pine. Angus sat down in the snow to watch what Mister did while Sadie jumped around, biting at the snow and trying to throw it back up into the sky from which it had fallen. Mister unwrapped the white thing from around his neck to set it down on the ground, and still Toaff had no idea what it might be. Then Mister took one end and reached up, to the tip of the fir.

When Mister started winding the white thing around the fir tree, Toaff had even less idea what was going on. He sat and watched and could only wait and see. Eventually Mister led the dogs back by the chestnut tree, dragging the end of the long white thing behind him. Sadie jumped on it and grabbed it in her teeth and shook it until Mister said something unfriendly and Angus yarked, "Stoppit! Not a *yark!*" She dropped it and the three of them walked back through the snow toward the nest-house, the long white thing trailing after. They crossed the stone wall just below where Toaff sat watching.

"Squirrel?" Sadie yarked up, but Toaff didn't like to answer when Mister and Angus were there. "Tomorrow?" Sadie yarked, but he kept quiet. "Tomorrow," she said, and followed Angus across to the white nest-house. Tomorrow would be just fine for Toaff.

By then it was too dark for Toaff to go find out what Mister had been doing. Besides, the wind was picking up. He didn't think the wind was bringing a storm, but because there had not yet been a storm, he hadn't learned how a snowstorm smelled different from ordinary snow, so he stayed where he was, sniffing the air, listening to the wind, watching. All the entrances to the nest-house shone yellow. The air lay still and dark over the pasture. The fir tree—

All at once lights burst out in the fir tree. Lights were scattered all through it, hidden along its branches, buried in among its needles, as if the fir was growing lights, not cones. The lights gleamed white, like shining flakes of snow that never finished falling. Toaff had never seen anything like that, a tree full of lights. He stared and wondered and enjoyed and didn't know, all at the same time.

In not very long, he would put his head into his warm den and call Soaff out to see it; and the next time he saw Nilf, he would tell the little Churrchurr about it; and if he listened carefully, he was pretty sure Sadie could tell him the word for those lights. Then all four of them, however different they all were, each one from all the other ones, could know the same word.

Toaff ran back along the branch, to bring Soaff out to see this new and surprising and wonderful thing.

# ABOUT THE AUTHOR

Cynthia Voigt is the author of many fine books for young readers. Her honors include a Newbery Medal for *Dicey's Song* (Book 2 in the Tillerman Cycle), a Newbery Honor for *A Solitary Blue* (Book 3 in the Tillerman Cycle), and the Margaret A. Edwards Award for Outstanding Literature for Young Adults. For younger readers, her books include the Mister Max trilogy, *Teddy & Co.*, and two other books set on the same farm as *Toaff's Way: Young Fredle* and *Angus and Sadie*.

Cynthia Voigt lives on an island in Maine. You can read more about her books at CynthiaVoigt.com.

# ABOUT THE ILLUSTRATOR

Sydney Hanson was raised in Minnesota alongside numerous pets. Her illustrations and paintings still reflect her love for animals and the natural world. Her books include *Panda Pants* by Jacqueline Davies and *How Do You Take a Bath?* by Kate McMullan.

Sydney lives in Los Angeles. You can visit her at sydwiki.tumblr.com.